Little Warrior

Boy Patriot of Georgia

D1417201

Patriot Kids of the American Revolution Series

Book Two

To Caleb,
HUZZAH!

GEOFF BAGGETT

DEDICATION

To my brand new grandson and Sons of the American Revolution Compatriot, Jackson Hunter Baggett. I hope he loves doing living history as much as I do. I have a cocked hat and weskit waiting for him.

Cover Design by Natasha Show - natashasnow.com

GEOFF BAGGETT

UNDERSTANDING THE TIMES

The British and their Redcoat soldiers were not the only enemies of the Patriot cause in the American Revolution. Indeed, not all soldiers in the conflict wore colorful red or blue uniforms. Throughout the years of the conflict the British made alliances with various Native American tribes along the frontier. The Iroquois, Creek, Cherokee, Chickasaw, and Shawnee tribes, among others, took part in combat against American forces. There were also many citizens of the Americas who took the side of the British. They were known as Loyalists, or were sometimes called Tories. Sometimes neighbors fought against one another in the war, especially in the South.

Many Patriots were ordinary men and women who simply defended their families and homes along the frontier against those Loyalist (Tory) forces and their Native American allies. This is a fictional story about one of those families ... the Robert Hammock family of Virginia and Georgia. They were a real family of the 1700's. They lived during a very difficult time and had to fight for their security and freedom.

This book deals with several difficult themes. You will read about the war, violence, guns, Native Americans (called Indians in the 18th Century), and slavery. These things were part of everyday life on the frontier during the American Revolution. Check the glossary in the back if you have difficulty with any "Revolutionary War words."

There are several descriptions of battles and war in this book, as well. These things must be included so that you can have a true understanding of the period of the Revolutionary War. If you have questions about these things or if they trouble you, I encourage you to talk to your parents or another responsible adult in your life. Ask them questions. Learn about your history!

Geoff Baggett

GEOFF BAGGETT

Part I

1774 - The Trek to Georgia

CHAPTER ONE
A GREAT ADVENTURE!

Lewis Hammock sighed and sat impatiently atop his horse. He was so very tired of waiting. And he was doing everything that he could to avoid getting caught up in the tearful goodbyes that were in his immediate future.

It was the spring of 1774 and Robert Hammock, Lewis's father, was taking his family away from their ancestral lands in Virginia on a quest to claim frontier land and establish a farm in the faraway colony of Georgia.

Lewis was ready to get on with the trip. This was shaping up to be the greatest adventure that he could ever imagine. Even though he was only nine years old, his father was allowing him to ride his own horse! All of the other children had to ride with their mother in the wagon.

But it wasn't just the horse and riding the trails like a grown-up that excited Lewis so. He looked down and patted the Virginia long rifle that lay across his lap. He rubbed the handles of the flintlock pistols that were attached to his saddle. His father had entrusted him with powerful weapons. Lewis was being counted on to defend his family from bandits, robbers, and marauding Indians! What an adventure, indeed!

Lewis cast a glance toward his Papa, who stood talking to Lewis's grandfather, Robert Jackson. Grandpa Robert and Grandma Abigail had come to see them off on their journey. They were heartbroken to see their daughter, Milly, leaving home and riding off into the wild Indian lands of Georgia. Lewis's mother and grandmother were both busy crying their eyes out.

Yep! Lewis had about all of this nonsense that he could stand. He gathered a little bit of courage and them cleared his throat. "Isn't it time to go, Papa? We have a long way to travel."

His father shot him an angry look. "Lewis, it will be time to go when I say that it's time to go. Now mind your manners. A boy your age needs to be seen, but not heard. You will do well to remember that."

"Yes, Papa," Lewis mumbled.

He sat quietly and amused himself by blowing out his breath and watching the condensation form a white cloud in the crisp spring air. He also eavesdropped on his father's conversation.

Lewis's grandpa asked his son-in-law, "Robert, is everything in order in the house?"

"Yes, sir," Robert responded. "The cabin is clear. It's all ready for the new owners to move right in."

Robert's declaration about the empty house caused Milly Hammock to break down into sorrowful tears. Lewis hated to see her so upset, but his patience was beginning to wear thin. He wondered, "How can anyone be so attached to this rickety, drafty old cabin?"

Lewis's father tried to comfort his mother. "Milly, darling, everything is going to be all right."

"I know it is, Robert. I have faith in God and faith in you. It just hurts to think of someone else living in our home … the place where we have lived so long and raised our children."

Robert smiled and wiped a tear from her cheek with his thumb. He stared deeply into her blue eyes.

"It's just an old Virginia cabin, my love. And it's not even a very good one, at that! You know how cold and drafty it is in the winter and how that south roof leaked no matter how many times I fixed it. I almost feel bad selling it to Mr. Wilkes."

Milly giggled through her tears.

"We'll make a new home in Georgia. A bigger home and a nicer home, with lots of land for our boys and girls to roam."

Lots of land to roam! How Lewis liked the sound of that! His mind wandered to visions of rabbits, squirrels, deer, and elk. He reached down and rubbed the cool barrel of his trusty rifle. He smiled and thought, "Look out, Georgia, here I come!"

Lewis's mother buried her head into her husband's chest as he hugged her tightly. Lewis's grandmother, standing behind her, wept even more loudly.

Edward Jackson snatched his wife over to him. "Now, woman, that'll be enough of that frightful racket! You're terrifying these poor children. Stop that confounded wailing and love on these kids. It may be a long time before you see them again."

Well ... that was definitely the wrong thing to say, for it started a brand new chorus of weeping from the emotional woman. Lewis's grandma broke away from her husband with great drama and began gathering her grandchildren.

"Lewis, get down from that huge horse and hug me! Robert, Joshua, John ... come to me boys. Come and hug your grandmother, for I fear that I shall most certainly never see any of you again!"

Lewis rolled his eyes and dutifully climbed down from his horse. He handed his rifle to his father and walked over to his grandmother. He reluctantly endured her warm hugs and wet kisses.

Edward Jackson turned his attention away from his emotional wife and focused on his son-in-law, trying to ignore the storm of female emotion that raged behind him.

"Robert, have you decided upon your route of travel to Georgia?"

"Yes, sir. I've agonized over the decision all winter long. The new settlement lands in Georgia are northwest of Savannah, inland along the river. The great wagon road down through Hillsboro and Charlotte would be much shorter and a much more direct route, but it is also much more dangerous. It goes through untamed country and is a little too close to the Cherokee Indian lands for my comfort."

"So you're going on the King's Highway along the Atlantic coast, then?" inquired Edward.

"Yes, sir. It will add many miles and days to our journey, but it will be through settled territory and much safer."

His father-in-law nodded his approval. "I believe that is the right decision, Robert. The King's Highway is patrolled by both the British soldiers and the local militias. There are far fewer bandits and highwaymen than there were a few years ago. There are ample supplies along the route and plenty of civilized towns for you to stay in as you travel."

Lewis, still listening in on the adult conversation, heard several tantalizing words from his father ... British soldiers, militia, bandits, highwaymen. He could barely control his excitement!

"Yes, sir," agreed Robert. "There should be restaurants and boarding houses in Denton, New Bern, and Wilmington, to be sure. The entire South Carolina coast is thoroughly settled. I'm quite sure we'll be camping most of the way, but it will be nice to take a break and sleep in an actual bed every now and then. We should also be able to link up with other settlers headed south."

"I only wish that you had more armed men and guns for your security," lamented the older gentleman.

"Frank and I will be just fine. And Lewis can shoot a gun if he has to."

Lewis's grandfather made a disgusted face when he heard Frank's name. Grandfather Jackson did not like Frank. Frank was the family's African slave.

Frank was fourteen years old. He was the only slave that Robert Hammock owned ... but it was not because he actually wanted to own a slave. Robert's grandfather died in 1765 and left the boy to him as part of his estate. Robert sort of had no choice in the matter. Frank was a small child at the time, only five years old. He was orphaned as a baby and raised by another family in the slave quarters. When Robert's grandfather, Hugh Lambert, died, he left the little boy to Robert as part of his estate.

That was nine years ago. During that time Frank grew up in Robert and Milly's home and was more like a son to them than he was a slave. He definitely played the role of "big brother" for all of the younger Hammock children. Frank was a beloved and important member of the Hammock household.

Frank was Lewis's best friend. They were hunting buddies and enjoyed spending time together. Frank was a skilled hunter, an excellent shot, and a hard worker. Lewis looked up to Frank.

Robert's father-in-law stared disapprovingly at Frank, who stood leaning against the wagon. Frank's floppy hat was flipped up in the front, revealing the distinguished features of his dark brown face. His tall Brown Bess musket was resting against the wagon at his side. Leather straps of various sizes crossed his chest. He had a matching set of flintlock pistols tucked into his leather waist belt. The handles of each pistol barely peeked out of the opening of his dark blue coat. The young black man was quite an imposing and impressive sight.

"I'm not sure how I feel about you arming your slave. I do not believe it to be appropriate for him to carry weapons."

"Why is it not appropriate?" challenged Robert.

"Good God, man! He's an African slave! He's property! That boy could kill you all in your sleep and run off into the night!"

That notion made Robert laugh out loud.

Lewis, still being bombarded by vigorous hugs from his grandmother, chuckled as well. He shook his head and thought, "Grandpa Jackson doesn't know what he's talking about. The notion that Frank would ever hurt us. Ha!"

Robert responded, "Now who is being dramatic, Edward? That is absolutely absurd! I've known Frank since he was a baby. He's like a son to me."

"That slave boy is most definitely not your son!" exclaimed the emotional, offended grandfather.

"No, not by blood. But by sweat and time and affection, he's just like a son to me. I know him as well as I know all of my boys. I don't view him as a slave, and I'll never treat him like a slave. The moment that he ever wants to leave our family I will gladly give him his papers and his freedom. I trust him with my life ... with my wife and children's lives. You can rest assured that we are all in good hands with Frank on the trigger of a musket."

"I still don't like it ... guns and slaves," Edward mumbled.

"Well, you don't have to like it. But it suits our family just fine."

The older man realized his defeat. He quietly nodded his agreement.

"Look, Edward, I don't want us to depart on bad terms. You've been good to us. Your gift of this land, your unwavering support, and your friendship have meant everything to this family. We could not have made it without you. But it's come time for us to move on and to do so on our own terms."

"I know it is time, Robert. I could tell that you've been growing restless for quite a while now. I know that you will all be just fine, and that you will do well for yourself down in Georgia. But I'm going to miss all of you."

The older gentleman broke down into silent tears. Robert gently patted his shoulder.

"We'll not be that far, Edward. We'll be just three weeks' ride away. Perhaps you and Abigail can come down for a visit soon."

Edward Jackson shook his head. "No, son, my traveling days are over. I'm too old. I can barely come up with the strength to leave my own farm these days. I certainly don't want to stray very far from my own bed. No, I suspect that Abigail is right … this is the last time that I will see any of you."

"I hate it when you speak that way, Edward. It all sounds so final. I feel a tremendous burden of guilt for causing this separation."

His father-in-law wiped his eyes with the sleeve of his dark green linen coat. "Now, Robert, don't you fret the whining of an old man. Young families have left home for opportunity and adventure since the dawn of time. I'm quite sure my emotions are the same ones experienced by our own ancestors as they watched their sons and daughters and grandchildren board ships in London and Liverpool bound for America. It is always difficult to watch our loved ones go, yet it is also difficult to blame them for wanting to go."

"It's still hurts, doesn't it?" remarked Robert.

"Indeed it does, son. Indeed it does." Edward Jackson winked at him and leaned closer. "But if I was just twenty years younger and my wife wasn't so ornery, I'd be hitching up my wagon and going, too."

Robert chuckled and winked at his father-in-law. He whispered, "I would welcome you in my caravan and in my camp, Edward. But Miss Abigail … not so much."

Both men laughed and embraced one another, slapping one another on the back with affection. They separated after lingering a few moments.

Robert looked at his wife and sons, locked in the embrace of his mother-in-law. "Milly … boys, say your final farewells. It is time for us to depart. We have many miles to travel."

The youngsters didn't need any further instruction. They broke free from their grandmother with little emotion or fanfare and raced for the back of the wagon. The three youngest boys clamored into the rear, eager to begin their adventure.

Lewis ran back to his horse and pulled himself up onto the huge animal's back. He almost looked comical ... a scruffy nine-year-old perched atop such a huge, majestic animal. What was not comical was the pair of pistols strapped across the pommel of his English saddle. His father handed him his .36 caliber flintlock rifle, which he comfortably balanced across his lap.

Milly walked over to the wagon. She handed little Nancy to Frank. He balanced the little girl on his hip with his left arm and held out his hand to assist Milly up onto the seat of the wagon. Nancy spontaneously grabbed Frank's face and pulled his cheek to her lips, planting a slobbery kiss and squealing with delight. Frank grinned his brilliantly white, toothy grin as he handed the little girl to her mother and then mounted the seat of the wagon beside them.

Robert climbed nimbly up onto his horse and guided the animal to the side of the wagon nearest his wife. Lewis took his position behind the wagon.

Robert nodded to the older couple. "Edward, Abigail, we are grateful to both of you for you seeing us off today. I trust that we will see one another again very soon."

"We pray God's mercies for your travel and for your future, Robert," responded Edward. "Take good care of our girls and boys."

Robert leaned over and extended his hand to his father-in-law. "I promise that I will, Edward. We will write you as soon as we arrive in Georgia, won't we Milly?"

His wife wiped her tears and adjusted her bonnet. "Yes, dear. Of course we will. And sooner, perhaps.

Mother, I will attempt to send letters and notes from some of the cities along our route, if you would like me to."

"Oh, yes, my dear!" exclaimed her mother. "Please tell us all about your travels and keep us informed of your progress. It will enable us to pray more diligently for all of you."

"Very well then, Mother. I will write you at every possible opportunity."

Her mother stumbled forward to the wagon and took her daughter's hand. "Go with God, my dear. I shall forever love you with all of my heart."

"And I shall always love you, dear Mother."

Edward Jackson interrupted the endearments, "Well, off you go, then, Hammock family! To the wild woods of Georgia! Enjoy your adventure, and live your lives to the fullest. We will see you in the Hereafter, if not sooner."

"Thank you, Edward. Be blessed, my friend," responded Robert.

"And you, as well, Robert."

With the family blessing received, Robert Hammock clucked at his horse and trotted slowly down the road. Frank gave a quick snap of the reins and launched the wagon, falling in behind Robert. Lewis brought up the rear, following behind the two horses tethered to the back of the heavily loaded wagon.

Three beaming faces shined in the rear opening of the wagon. The little Hammock boys all extended their hands through the opening, shouting, "Goodbye, Grandmother! Goodbye, Grandfather!"

Lewis turned on his horse and waved once, and then turned his attention back to the road before him. He needed to keep his eyes open for Indians and bandits, after all! He had big responsibilities on this dangerous trek.

Edward and Abigail Jackson stood in the muddy, rutted road and held one another, weeping openly as they watched Lewis and his horse disappear around the bend in the road.

Sadly, like Grandpa Jackson predicted, it really was the last time that they would ever see their daughter, Milly, and her family.

CHAPTER TWO
SWAMPS, RIVERS, AND BIG CITIES

Three days later the Hammock family located a camp along the King's Highway that was said to be occupied by other families who were traveling south to Georgia. There were three wagons in the small field. They headed toward a young couple camped beside the nearest wagon. The man was pouring water over the ashes of his campfire. The young woman, who looked to be no more than seventeen or eighteen years old, cradled a baby in her arms.

Lewis walked over with his father to meet them.

Robert spoke first. "Good morning! Are you folks preparing to head south?"

The young man nodded. "That we are, sir. Headed for Georgia to claim a farm on some of that new Indian land."

"As are we," responded Robert. He motioned toward the other two wagons in the field. "And the others?"

"They are Georgia-bound, as well. We are all set to leave within the hour."

"Good." Robert dismounted his horse and walked over to the young man. They shook hands. "My name is Robert Hammock. This is my eldest son, Lewis."

"I'm Christopher Chandler. This is my wife, Esther."

Robert tipped his hat to the woman, as did Lewis. "Madam, I am pleased to make your acquaintance."

Lewis mumbled, "Ma'am."

Robert asked Mr. Chandler, "Would you good folks mind if our family joined up with your group? We believe that there is greater safety in numbers on the King's Highway."

"As do we, Mr. Hammock. You are most welcome to join us." The young man glanced over Robert's shoulder at the Hammock wagon. "Is that your slave?"

"Yes. His name is Frank. My grandfather gave him to me when he was a small boy. I raised him in my home with my own children. He is a trusted servant and friend. Why do you ask? Is it a problem?"

"No, Mr. Hammock. No problem. I've just not had much exposure to the whole slavery business. I've not been around a lot of slaves."

"Well, Mr. Chandler —"

"Call me Chris."

"Well ... Chris ... I'm not really an advocate of slavery, either. I simply inherited Frank. He is an excellent horseman and hunter, and is quite skilled with both musket and pistol. He will be an asset on this journey, I can assure you."

Chris grinned in response. "Of that I have no doubt. Why don't you let me introduce you to the other families? We should be ready to move out in just a short while."

"Sounds good," responded Robert.

A half-hour later, after all of the introductions were made, the small convoy of wagons eased onto the rutted King's Highway and headed southward. Robert agreed that his family would take the lead of their tiny wagon train. He and Lewis led the convoy on horseback. Chris Chandler's wagon brought up the rear of the column.

By noontime the appearance of the land began to change. The low crop land soon gave way to swamps and bogs. The road narrowed significantly as thick trees and vines crept in upon its edges. The air became filled with a rich, sweet stench of water and decay. Soon black, stagnant water came right up to the left side of the slightly elevated roadway. Huge cypress trees with knobby roots grew straight and tall out of the water.

Then hordes of mosquitoes descended upon them. The bugs swarmed in huge, buzzing, stinging clouds. The travelers were on the edge of a huge swamp.

Lewis slapped at the bugs that coated his skin. Mosquitoes were flying up his nose and into his mouth. He accidentally swallowed a mouthful of them! The most annoying and painful ones flew down deep into his ear, stinging him on the inside. It was absolutely unbearable.

"Papa!" he exclaimed. "I cannot stand all of these bugs! How are we ever going to survive this?"

"I know it's bad, son. It can't last forever. I'm going to check on your mother and the little ones."

Robert slowed his horse and pulled back beside the wagon.

"Is everyone all right?" he asked.

Milly exhaled in frustration as she swatted the air in front of her face. "We're being eaten alive by these horrid bugs, Robert. What is this place?"

"My dear, this is what is known as the Great Dismal Swamp."

"Goodness, that sounds horrible! How far does it go?"

"We travel along the western border of it for about forty miles. You'd better get used to it for now. We are going to be near this swamp for a couple of days. We'll have to make camp beside it tonight."

The loud moans and wails of his other sons emanated from beneath the cover of the wagon.

Milly shook her head. "I don't know if I can stand being feasted upon by these bugs for two whole days."

"We'll see if we can do something to help chase them away once we make camp. Just try to keep the children covered up as much as possible. We don't want them getting swamp fever."

So the group trudged along, moving at a steady and deliberate pace. The road meandered away from the swamp, itself, but the air remained musty and humid. There was no escaping the humidity or the bugs. The road crossed several small creeks, requiring crossings at shallow fords.

Camp that first night, so close to the insect-infestedswamp, was nothing short of miserable. The families brought their wagons in close and built several smoky fires in an attempt to drive the biting insects away. The mothers vigorously rubbed the skin of their children with a protective layer of soot and mud, but it had precious little affect upon the insect attack that descended upon them after the sun went down. The bugs attacked without mercy throughout the night.

Lewis buried himself beneath his wool blanket, but the heat was unbearable. He tried to cover all of his skin that he could and only leave his mouth exposed so that he could breathe, but the mosquitoes bit him on his lips. He barely slept at all.

The men finally gave up and roused their families two hours before dawn. They ate a cold breakfast, and proceeded southward as quickly as possible.

It was noon when they finally made their way clear of the worst of the swamplands. The little convoy rolled into the North Carolina village of Edenton shortly before nightfall. After a few inquiries Robert located a bath house and a place to board his family for the night. The other families in the convoy sought similar comforts.

The woman who operated the tavern and boarding house even had a soothing local remedy for the bug bites. It was an herbal medicine that Robert had never heard of. It worked wonders. Robert did not bother to inquire about its ingredients. He was just glad that it seemed to ease the itching.

The next morning Robert splurged and bought his family a hot meal at a small tavern. Afterward they felt thoroughly rejuvenated and refreshed for the journey.

The four families met south of town at noon and continued their journey toward Georgia. They steadily made their way across the rivers and streams and through the fields, hamlets, and villages of North Carolina.

One week after their departure from Edenton the weary travelers forded the Neuse River and rode into the port city of New Bern, North Carolina's colonial capital.

New Bern was, by far, the most beautiful, modern, and wealthy place that Robert had ever seen. Red-coated British troops were everywhere. Hundreds of them marched in the streets and populated camps just outside the city.

The amazing display of wealth in New Bern was a major shock for the Virginians. The women and children of the group stared at the spectacle with their mouths wide open. Robert was overwhelmed.

Lewis broke the strange silence, "I've never seen anything like this, Papa. Do all the people down here in the Carolinas live so fancy like this?"

Robert chuckled, "No, son. This place is definitely not normal. It is New Bern, a port city and the British capital of North Carolina. Money flows in and out of this town like a mighty river. So don't get too used to what you're seeing. Georgia won't be anything like this at all, I assure you."

"I didn't think so," responded Lewis. He was glad. The city seemed very odd to him. He was anxious to get back out into the countryside. After all, there were no dangerous Indians or bandits in the city!

Milly's voice called from the wagon behind them, "Robert, can we stay here in New Bern for a while? We haven't seen a bed or a bath in over a week now. It would be wonderful to wash off this swamp grime and river mud. Your children are beginning to stink!"

"Yes, my love. I quite agree that some hot water and a dry bed would be nice. Let me check with the others and see what their plans are."

Robert guided his horse back along the short convoy to collaborate with the other three families. The Englers, Germans from Pennsylvania, were a bit reluctant to stop. However, they finally agreed that one day of rest would be good for the entire group. The men agreed to stay in New Bern for two nights. Soon each family headed off in their separate directions in search of lodging.

Robert and Lewis easily located a nice tavern with two second-floor boarding rooms available. While Frank secured their wagons and mounts at a nearby livery, Robert paid for both available rooms for his family and then took the entire brood a half-block east to find a laundry and bath house. He had to make special arrangements for Frank, but that only took a couple of extra shillings. Frank bathed at a nearby outdoor establishment for slaves and freedmen. Robert also gave Frank the money to pay his own lodging in the hayloft of the livery stable.

Two hours later the Hammocks had clean bodies, clean clothes, and a healthy appetite. They satisfied their hunger with a hearty beef stew and loaves of dry bread at the tavern. They washed down their meal with mugs full of frothy milk. The Hammocks tumbled joyfully into their rented beds shortly after sundown and slept for almost twelve hours.

The family met Frank the next morning and took several hours touring the sites of New Bern and stocking up on a few extra supplies. They enjoyed the mid-day meal at a seafood place near the docks. The establishment served a gray-brown seafood stew and fresh fish grilled over an open fire. Food from the ocean was a new experience for the Hammocks, and it was a tasty event that they would not soon forget. After the meal they sat around a large outdoor table, sipping hot tea.

"What shall we do this afternoon?" inquired Robert.

"These children and I need a nap," responded Milly. "But you men-folk feel free to do as you wish."

Frank spoke up, "If it's all right Mr. Robert, I would like to go a few blocks west of here and look around. I hear there's a large freedman's village on that side of town. I would like to go see what is there and meet some of the local folk. I might even get some island or African food there."

"Of course, Frank. That's just fine. I can well understand your desire to go and be among some of your own people."

"I'm most grateful, Mr. Robert."

"Can I go with Frank?" asked Lewis.

"Well … I think Frank might want some time alone. I'm not so sure that you would be very welcome where he is going."

Frank interjected, "Lewis is more than welcome to come with me, Mr. Robert. I would enjoy the company. I'll keep a close eye on him. He'll be just fine."

Robert seemed hesitant. "It's up to you, Frank. But I want you to be sure and take good care of my son."

"I will, Mr. Robert. You know you can count on me."

"Very well, then. You boys enjoy your afternoon, and I'll see you back at the tavern for supper."

The members of the Hammock family dispersed to their various places of interest. Lewis was thrilled to be going somewhere new and exciting with Frank. It did not take long for them to reach what was a distinctly African part of the town. Colorful cloths adorned dozens of small wood huts. The smell and color of the food and snacks for sale along the street were absolutely tantalizing.

Even though they had only recently finished their seafood dinner, the boys were still aching to try something new. They elected to stop at one particularly busy establishment to see if they could purchase some sweet treats. They sat down at a small table near the street, under the shade of a large tree. Moments later a rather large, loud, round-faced woman of African descent approached them.

"Well, now, this most definitely is a first for our humble business!" She spoke with a thick accent that neither Frank nor Lewis recognized. "Here we have a young white mastah and as finely dressed a slave mahn as I have ever in my life seen. Just look at those fine breeches and coat. And that beautiful, expensive fur felt hat! My, oh my! You two young ones are surely not from New Bern."

Lewis spoke up, "No ma'am. We're from Virginia. And I'm no one's master. My name is Lewis Hammock and this is my big brother, Frank. We're headed to Georgia and just stopped here in town for a rest." He paused and then inquired, "Where are you from, anyway? You talk funny."

The fat woman placed both hands on her hips and then threw her head back, emitting a loud and boisterous laugh.

"You can call me Mama Anna. I'm from Jamaica, the most beautiful island in all the world. But I came to America to have my own business. And whatever do you mean, your big brutha? Now that is funny, boy! How I would like to have a look at yo mama and papa!"

She threw her head back again and laughed loudly.

Frank smiled broadly and spoke up, "Actually, madam, I am a slave. I belong to young Lewis's father. Lewis and his younger siblings do look up to me to be like a big brother."

"And just listen to you!" the woman exclaimed. "You don't just look the part of the gentleman, but you sound like one, as well! You sound like one of those educated Englishmen that stumbles in here from time to time. Now tell me, fine gentlemen, how may I serve you today?"

"We want something sweet!" Lewis responded enthusiastically. "Mama and Papa made me eat some of that ocean stew for dinner. But I want some dessert."

Frank nodded his agreement, "I, too, would enjoy some dessert. What do you recommend from your kitchen?"

The woman threw back her head and cackled again. "I cannot get over those words of yours, boy. You don't sound like no slave I ever heard before."

"Yes, madam. Now ... about the possibility of dessert?"

She quickly composed herself. "Of course, sir. Well, let me serve you some African sweets that you will not soon forget. I will bring you both a sampling of my sweet rice pudding with raisins and nutmeg, brown sugar candied yams, and a slice of tasty watermelon. How does that sound?"

"Delicious!" exclaimed Lewis.

"And would you, by chance, have any coffee?" inquired Frank.

"Of course. I will bring you both a cup of my rich Jamaican coffee, extra sweet with lots of cream."

"Splendid," responded Frank.

That one word from Frank began yet another cascade of hearty laughter from the woman. She cackled and shook her head as she walked toward the kitchen to fetch their food.

A few minutes later she returned with two plates of beautiful sweet delights and two steaming cups of sweet coffee. Frank and Lewis talked, laughed, and savored every morsel of the deliciously sweet and exotically spiced food. As the mealtime crowd began to die down, Mama Anna and some of the other workers stopped by their table to chat and ask questions about their journey to Georgia.

Lewis thoroughly enjoyed all of the attention and the wonderful company. But soon it was time to go. Frank had other things in the freedman village that he wanted to see. He paid their bill and bid the extremely entertaining women a very gentlemanly farewell.

The boys had walked barely a half-block from the café when a loud voice with a thick English accent called out nearby, "You, boy! Come over here immediately!"

Both Lewis and Frank looked around. They saw four British soldiers standing near a doorway to a building across the street. The soldiers seemed to be looking in their direction.

"They're not talking to us, are they?" asked Lewis.

"I don't see why they would be talking to us," responded Frank. Both boys shrugged and resumed their slow amble down the street.

"I'm speaking to you, you fancy African baboon!"

Frank and Lewis turned to see one of the soldiers, a rather short fellow, marching angrily toward them. He held a shiny Brown Bess musket menacingly across his chest. It seemed that he was, indeed, addressing Frank.

"I'm sorry, were you speaking to me?" inquired Frank.

"I see no other fancy African baboons in the vicinity. Yes, you big dummy, I am speaking to you. You will accompany me this instant to our warehouse. We have an army wagon that needs to be unloaded."

Frank was somewhat at a loss for words, and not quite sure how to respond. "I'm sorry, sir, but I am not available to assist you today. I have business to attend to and I am responsible for this lad."

The soldier's head spun around and he stepped forward in a confrontational pose. He drew his face close to Frank's, bumping the forward fold of his black cocked hat into Frank's nose. The man screamed, almost hysterically, "You have no business other than the King's business, you ignorant slave! Now come along, boy. That wagon is not going to unload itself."

Frank paused. "Sir, I don't think you understand … I am not a resident of this town. I am a traveler passing through on my way to — "

He never got another word out. The soldier brought the stock of the musket upwards in a swift motion, striking

Frank firmly in the lower jaw. The force of the blow spun Frank to his right. He was momentarily dazed and suddenly light-headed. He dropped to his knees, cradling his jaw in his hands. An instant later the soldier drove the stock of the musket down squarely onto the top of Frank's head, knocking him all the way to the ground.

Lewis covered Frank's body with his own and screamed, "Stop it! You have no right to do this!"

"Get out of here, boy! I am a King's soldier, and have every right to do as I see fit to serve the Crown. It is you stupid colonials who have no rights. Now be gone … unless you want to be introduced to my musket, as well."

Lewis dropped to his knees beside Frank. "Frank, are you all right?" Lewis wept.

Frank's eyes fluttered open. His jaw was strangely out of place, obviously broken or dislocated from its socket. He managed to mumble from his swollen, open mouth, "Go …. find … your father …" His eyes fluttered and then closed as he slipped into unconsciousness.

CHAPTER THREE
REDCOATS

Lewis hid fearfully behind his father. They were standing in the British commander's office at a military jail outside the city. Lewis had never seen his father so angry before.

Robert Hammock was in a blind rage. He slammed his fist on the desk that stood between him and the British major. The officer's empty teacup jumped from its saucer and wobbled awkwardly across the desk. His beautifully carved name plate, identifying him as *"Maj. Thos. Dowling,"* tumbled off of the small stack of books upon which it previously rested.

"Major Dowling, this is absolutely outrageous!" he shouted. "I demand that you release my slave from custody immediately and that the soldier who assaulted him be brought up on charges!"

The major stood slowly and leaned forward, placing his weight on the knuckles of his fists upon the desktop.

The officer growled, "Sir, I strongly suggest that you change your tone, or I will have you thrown into the cell with your slave. I am the King's representative and commander of this facility, and you will address me

23

accordingly. I will not tolerate such abuse in my own headquarters."

Robert sucked in a deep breath and attempted to compose himself. "I sincerely apologize, Major. I am attempting to control my emotions. But I am simply finding it difficult to understand how a fifteen-year-old slave and a nine-year-old lad could receive such violent treatment from a soldier of the British army! They were simply walking down the street, enjoying a peaceful afternoon, and minding their own business."

The officer seemed unimpressed.

"That is not the account that I received from Corporal Ames." The major reached toward his desk and picked up a piece of paper. "According to his official report, Corporal Ames says that he approached the slave and ordered him to accompany him to an adjacent warehouse to unload a wagon. He reports that the slave refused his command, and then he became angry and threatened the corporal's safety, upon which time the corporal was forced to defend himself."

The major sat back down in his chair and removed his spectacles, dropping them on the desk. "The corporal claims that he acted to protect his own life in the face of a violent physical threat from your slave."

"Frank poses no threat to your soldiers, or to anyone for that matter."

"Oh, really?" responded the major. "Then can you explain these?"

He reached into a desk drawer to his right and pulled out Frank's pistols, dropping them loudly upon the desktop.

"My men tell me that your slave was preparing to draw these pistols and fire them."

Lewis could remain silent no longer. He almost screamed, "That's an absolute lie, Papa! Frank never threatened anybody, and he sure didn't draw a pistol on those four soldiers! His coat was all buttoned up and closed! They must've found those pistols on him after I ran to get you!"

"Mind your tongue, Lewis!" scolded his father. "This is an adult conversation."

"But Papa, it's all a lie! A horrible, terrible lie! Frank was just trying to explain to the soldier that we were visitors from out of town and passing through to Georgia when he hit him with the stock of his musket! He just up and smacked Frank in the jaw! Frank never even saw it coming!"

The officer sneered, "Mr. Hammock, it seems that you need to learn to control your children, as well as your slaves."

"He's just trying to set the record straight, Major. He was, after all, an eyewitness to these events."

"Indeed. But as you and I both know, neither the word of a child nor the testimony of a slave bears any credence in such matters. I have the sworn report of a soldier of the King. That is sufficient for me, and for the law."

"So the word of a lawful British citizen of the Americas holds no weight whatsoever against a piece of paper written by a man in a red coat?"

The officer chuckled, retorting haughtily, "I dare say, sir, that you have never set foot in England. You are certainly no British citizen. You are simply one of our wayward American children … a mere subject, nothing more. You serve the King and Crown at our leisure and good pleasure."

Robert was aghast. He did not know how to respond. He had always considered himself a loyal citizen of Great Britain, a servant of the King, and under the protection of British law. This British officer had just shattered his lifelong beliefs. Surely this major did not speak for all officers in the King's army!

"Frankly, Major, I cannot believe that I am hearing such deeply insulting words from a British officer."

The major lifted one eyebrow. "Insulting, perhaps, but certainly not surprising. There is a stench of rebellion in America, Mr. Hammock. Massachusetts is aflame with it, aggravated by a band of outlaws who call themselves "Sons of Liberty." Now there are rumblings of an unlawful legislature ... a Continental Congress ... taking form somewhere up North in the coming months. We must crush these seeds of rebellion immediately and get you colonials back to doing what you are here to do ... providing the goods and services needed by the King and Great Britain."

"I assure you, Major, that I have always been a loyal subject of the Crown. I know nothing of the rebellion of which you speak," proclaimed Robert.

Pointing at the pistols, the officer screamed, "Then you will explain these weapons to me!" He pounded his fist on his desk to show his seriousness.

"They are for our family's protection, nothing more."

"In the hands of a slave?" inquired the major, incredulously.

"Yes, sir. Frank is, indeed, my slave. But he is a trusted member of our household." Robert nodded toward Lewis. "My children are all very young. This boy is my oldest son, not old enough to assist me in defending the family. But Frank is an expert marksman. He hunts and helps feed our family. Recently we departed Virginia and embarked upon a journey of several hundred miles to settle on the Georgia frontier. It is a journey full of danger. Surely you understand the wisdom of an extra set of weapons for the protection of my family."

"Not in the hands of a slave. Law demands that he receive thirty-nine lashes of the whip for carrying a weapon. The presence of two pistols may, indeed, double that count," retorted the officer.

Lewis gasped when he heard the word, "lashes." Surely they would not beat Frank with a whip. Not thirty-nine times!

"Father, do something!" Lewis begged.

His father barked, "Silence, Lewis!" He turned to face the major.

"Sir, you cannot beat my slave for carrying my pistols with my permission!" Robert yelled, growing angrier by the minute. "Besides, you would not have even known about them had not your soldier interrupted my slave and my son in the middle of the street."

"I have already explained to you the sequence of events in the corporal's report."

Robert stood his ground. "And I have already explained to you that your corporal is a pathetic liar."

The major exhaled in exasperation. "You are testing my patience, Mr. Hammock."

"And my patience is already stretched beyond its limit, Major Dowling. Your men had no right to approach my slave, in the presence of my young son, on a public street and then demand forced labor without first consulting me, his rightful owner. It was your soldier's action that was unlawful."

The major turned his head and gazed out of his office window toward the street. There was a long period of awkward silence. He finally turned his eyes back to meet the glaring gaze of Robert Hammock. He exhaled a long, tired, defeated breath. Lewis held his breath. It seemed like the British officer was about to change his mind.

Major Dowling looked Robert in the eyes. "Mr. Hammock, this affair has already consumed more of my time than I had to spare. I will release the slave and the weapons to you and consider the matter closed. My only condition is that you take him and leave this city as rapidly as possible."

"Oh, you have nothing to worry about, Major. I cannot wait to shake the dust of this town off of my shoes," retorted Robert smartly. "But I believe that the speed of our departure will depend upon how much damage your men have inflicted upon my slave."

The major barked at a soldier who had been sitting silently at his desk in the corner of the room throughout the entire exchange, "Sergeant!"

"Sir!" responded the sergeant.

"Have the slave prisoner brought out to Mr. Hammock's wagon. He is to be released immediately."

"Right away, sir!"

The sergeant moved quickly, placing his white-trimmed black cocked hat on his head as he departed the office.

Robert stood tall and proud. "I would say, 'thank you,' Major, but I'm not exactly feeling grateful at this moment."

The officer did not even bother to look him in the eye. He merely began to shuffle papers on his desk. "That will be all, sir. Now kindly depart my office. Please close the door as you leave. And never come back."

"Gladly, but not before I get my pistols, Major."

The officer pushed the firearms across the desktop toward Robert, still refusing to make eye contact.

Robert didn't say another word. He grabbed the pistols with one hand and Lewis by the shoulder with his other hand and quickly left the building.

"Father, do we have to go get Frank somewhere?"

"No, Lewis, the soldiers will bring him to us in a moment. We will wait in the wagon."

Ten minutes later they heard the heavy clang of iron as a gate opened on the left edge of the courtyard. The sergeant from the office walked in front of the squad of soldiers that was transferring Frank. Two Redcoats dragged Frank between them. They held him by his arms. A cloth sack covered his head so that they could not see his face. He was not moving. Two other soldiers armed with muskets followed the two men dragging Frank.

Lewis exclaimed, "Frank!" He jumped from the wagon and began to run toward the soldiers.

"Stay where you are, boy!" commanded the sergeant. "Get back in your wagon. Mr. Hammock, you will remain in the wagon, as well. We will load your slave."

Lewis froze in fear for a moment, and then turned and ran back to the wagon. The sergeant lowered the rear board and the two soldiers who had been dragging Frank dumped him into the wagon bed as if he were a sack of potatoes. One of them chuckled as Frank moaned in pain.

Lewis leaned toward his father. "Papa, that's the one who hit Frank."

Almost on cue the corporal looked directly at Robert and grinned. He bragged in a thick, lower-class English accent, "Here's your uppity slave. He's a little worse for wear, but he'll be all right. I toughened him up for you a little bit, though."

Robert's faced turned crimson as his blood boiled with rage. Before he even realized what he was doing he jumped from the wagon seat and took three steps toward the tiny little corporal. The group of soldiers seemed a bit surprised at his sudden move, but none of them tried to stop him. Robert stared angrily at the corporal.

"Are you as tiny a little man on the inside as you are on the outside, Corporal Ames? Because only a little man could take such joy in abusing children and slave boys."

The corporal seemed surprised that the Colonial man would speak to him in such a way. He seemed downright disturbed that the man addressed him by name. His face flushed red in embarrassment and anger.

He shrieked in a loud rage, "You get back up on that seat right now, or that boy of yours will be driving the both of you home in the back of this wagon!"

"You don't scare me, little man. No matter how loud you get, you will always be just that … a tiny little excuse of a pathetic little man."

The sergeant interrupted the exchange, "Mr. Hammock, please get back in your wagon and depart the garrison. This matter is closed."

Robert glanced sideways at the sergeant and nodded. He tipped his hat, spun around, and jumped back into the seat of the wagon.

"Let's get out of here, Lewis."

Lewis slapped the reins and guided the team toward the gate. Two minutes later they were outside the compound. Lewis could feel the seat of the wagon shaking from his father's emotion and rage.

"Take the road to the left, Lewis."

His son obeyed. Robert noticed a small cluster of trees about a hundred yards up the highway.

"Park under the cover of those trees and let's take a look at Frank."

Again, Lewis obeyed. Robert dismounted the wagon before it reached a complete stop and ran around back to check on Frank. He climbed up into the wagon beside the injured boy and gently laid him over onto his back. He untied the string that secured the cloth sack over Frank's head and gently removed it. The sack did not come loose easily. Dried blood had caused the cloth to stick to the right side of his face.

Robert wasn't prepared for the sight that awaited him. Frank was almost unrecognizable. His chin was slightly ajar and shifted toward the left side of his face. The first upward blow from the musket stock had knocked his jaw out of its socket. The skin along his right jawbone had burst open from the blow. The break in his skin was the source of all of the blood that covered his face and clothing. Frank's bottom lip was huge, swollen until it looked like a large, ripe, purple plum.

All of those wounds could be fixed. What Robert was most concerned about was the blow to the top of his head. There was very little blood, but he could see considerable swelling of the top of his skull. This swelling, and the fact that Frank remained asleep, was what worried him the most. He prayed that Frank did not have a permanent injury to his brain.

Robert almost forgot that Lewis was with him. His son's small, frightened voice broke his concentration. "Is Frank all right, Papa?"

"I hope so, Lewis. I'm very worried about that huge knot on his head. It's been a couple of hours since he was hurt. He should be awake by now."

"Maybe he's just tired," commented Lewis, innocently.

Robert smiled at his son. "I'm sure he is. Can you fetch me a canteen of water? Let's see if we can wake him and clean him up just a bit."

Lewis jumped over the driver's seat and grabbed a wooden canteen from beneath the seat on the passenger side. He climbed up onto the side board of the wagon and handed it to his father. Robert popped the wood stopper from the canteen and gently poured the cool water over Frank's face. He coughed and gasped as the water ran over his nose and mouth, and then began swinging his arms and struggling to rise. He looked confused and very frightened.

Robert tried to calm him, "It's me, Frank! Everything's all right now. We got you out of that prison. Lewis is with me. See? He's right here."

Lewis jumped into the back of the wagon and knelt beside Frank's head. "I'm right here, Frank. Papa got you away from those nasty Redcoats. We're taking you back to Mama."

Robert saw the relief wash across Frank's face. The injured boy reached out with his left arm and pulled Lewis down to him, hugging him. He began to weep. And even though his mouth wouldn't move, he tried to talk. He literally pushed the words out of his mouth with his swollen tongue.

"I'm so sorry, Mr. Robert! I didn't mean to cause any trouble." His words were difficult to understand. His tears flowed freely and bloody slobber oozed from the corner of his swollen mouth. "I still don't understand what happened. That soldier hit me for no reason! I didn't do anything wrong, I swear!"

"Shhh ... hush now, Frank. I know you didn't do anything wrong. Don't you worry about it, now. It's all over. We're leaving this place and we're never coming back. I promise you that."

But Frank continued to weep. "I woke up right after they got me back to the jail. But then that man hurt me again."

Robert's face clouded. "Who hurt you again? That tiny fellow? That mean little corporal?"

Frank nodded. "The same one who clubbed me with that musket. Two of them held me up while he hit me in the belly and chest. He started with his fists, and finished with a wood club. It hurts to breathe."

Robert reached down and lifted Frank's bloody weskit and shirt from the waist of his breeches and looked at Frank's torso. He was badly bruised, especially on his left side. Robert had little doubt that some of his ribs were broken. There was no actual bleeding. Just tremendous swelling and deep, grotesquely purple bruising that showed through Frank's dark brown skin. Robert gently lowered the shirt to cover the wounds.

"Frank, I'm going to get you back to Milly. It'll take about fifteen minutes to make the trip to the boarding house. This British jail is way north of town. But I promise that I'll take it as slowly and gently as I possibly can."

"Thank you, Mr. Robert."

CHAPTER FOUR
THIEVES AND BANDITS

It was three days later before Frank was well enough to travel. While Frank was on the mend, Robert took the opportunity to replenish the family's supplies and gather information about the road to Georgia. Unfortunately, their convoy of friends followed their agreed-upon schedule and had already pressed on toward South Carolina. The Hammocks would be on their own.

When they finally departed New Bern, Robert intentionally maintained a slow pace. Frank rode in the back of the wagon, sleeping most of the time. Milly and the children constructed a soft pallet for him on the floor of the wagon and did everything possible to keep him comfortable. The family covered only fifteen to twenty miles per day, depending upon the condition of the road. Lewis drove the wagon and Robert stayed on horseback.

On the fourth day out of New Bern the air smelled strongly of salt water, and clouds of seagulls and other water birds filled the sky.

Lewis asked his father, "What's that strange smell, Papa?"

"It's salt, son. We must be pretty close to the sea."

33

"Can we go see it?"

Robert chuckled. "No, Lewis. Not yet. Even if we could find our way through this mass of brush, I doubt that we could get to the actual ocean. They say that North Carolina has narrow islands out on the far side of a great canal. The ocean is on the other side of those islands. You actually have to take a boat over there in order to visit the beach."

"Oh." Lewis looked heartbroken.

"Don't worry, Lewis. You'll see the ocean soon enough when we get into South Carolina. I believe that the King's Highway runs right along the open shore for many miles."

Lewis smiled and snapped the reins, pressing his team to the south.

The Hammock family pressed on. Two days later they passed through Wilmington, a large port city located on the Cape Fear River, near the southernmost coast of North Carolina. The road southwest of Wilmington was flat, wide, and hard-packed. It made for very easy traveling. Frank was obviously feeling better. He expressed his desire to get to work and get back to driving the wagon, but Robert insisted that he rest and recuperate for one more day. Toward mid-afternoon the air began to assume a musty, swampy odor.

Milly's sing-song voice pierced the silence of the afternoon, "It smells like that Dismal Swamp again, Robert. Please tell me that we are not headed into another one of those bug-infested places!"

Robert consulted a crude map that he had procured in New Bern. "No, my love, nothing quite so large as that swamp. We are, however, close to what is known as the Green Swamp. It is several miles to our right. I hope that the bugs will not be quite so bad."

Those words had just left his mouth when the first wave of mosquitoes and biting flies descended upon them. Milly glared at Robert in disgust.

Robert smiled grimly. "We'll just try to outrun these bugs and get past the swamp. Let's pick up the pace a bit."

He increased his horse to a light trot. Lewis snapped the leather reins and urged the team pulling the wagon to follow suit. They kept up the hard pace for almost an hour and a half. The stench of the swamp subsided, along with the attacking insects. Robert soon located a tall stand of pine trees just off of the highway. A clear, swift moving stream flowed nearby. It was a perfect camping spot. Evidence of previous campfires showed that the location had been used many times before.

"We'll stop here for the night," Robert announced. "This looks like a popular spot. It's nice and open, with plenty of water close by. We have a good hour of daylight left to make camp. How's Frank doing?"

Milly glanced through the opening in the canvas. "He's asleep again, Robert. I'm afraid that the injuries were much harder on him than he's been letting on. He's trying to act strong, but I think he's still suffering. The poor boy hasn't been awake much today."

"Maybe he'll be back to himself by morning," Robert prophesied wishfully. "We could sure use the help. Lewis has been doing a man's job these past couple of days."

"I'm doing just fine, Papa!" Lewis interjected. "I love driving the wagon!"

Robert smiled proudly at his boy. "I know you do son, and you've been doing a fine job. Now how about we take care of the horses and build a fire so your mother can get started on some supper?"

"Yes, Papa."

The family unpacked the necessary supplies from the wagon and prepared camp. The younger boys gathered firewood while Robert and Lewis tended to the horses, tethering them to a small bush beside the creek within reach of plenty of fresh grass to graze. Since it was a crisp, clear evening, Robert decided that they would "sleep out under the stars." In actuality, however, they would be sleeping under a very dense and high pine canopy. Mountains of fresh pine needles provided a bed that was more comfortable than anything they could find in a boarding house. Robert was looking forward to a very restful night.

An hour later, just as the sun was going down, Milly had supper ready. She had prepared a large pot of vegetable stew. It was a rich, creamy mixture of potatoes, carrots, and onions that was flavored with salt pork. There was an ample supply of dark, dry bread that they had purchased before leaving New Bern. Cool water and sweet, hot tea finished off the meal. Afterwards the family sat in the comfortable glow of the fire. Robert filled his clay pipe with tobacco and enjoyed a smoke while the children joined their mother in singing songs.

Little Robert called out to his father across the fire, "Papa, tell us a story!"

"Oh, you children have heard all of my stories," he replied.

"But you tell them so well, Papa. Please! Tell us again about Grandfather William and how he came across the great sea from England."

"You kids have heard that story a thousand times. Aren't you tired of it?"

The children responded with a chorus of encouragement. "Please, Papa. You tell it so well. Please tell it again!"

Robert sighed with joy. "Oh, all right then."

And for the next several minutes he recounted, one more time, the story of William O. Hammock's journey from England and his adventures on the high seas. He told about their ancestor's years of indentured servitude, a type of slavery in which a man signed his freedom away in order to gain passage on a ship. He described how William Hammock lived out his service along the coast of Virginia and how he was able to finally purchase his freedom. Then Robert told about how Grandfather William met his wife and grew a large family on the Virginia frontier.

The children knew the story so well that many times they finished his sentences for him. They clapped with glee when Robert finished his story about their family heritage. It was a familiar and joyous moment that they had shared many times around the hearth in their old Virginia cabin.

A deep voice from the darkness ended their joyful celebration. "That is an excellent story. Your family has a wonderful heritage."

Robert whipped his pistol from his belt as Lewis jumped for his rifle that was leaning against the wagon.

Again the voice spoke from the darkness. "You do not need your weapons. I mean your family no harm. I smelled your fire from a great distance away and I came in search of food and friendship."

"Are you alone?" Robert asked the intruder.

"Yes, I travel alone. I have been to the south, in what you call South Carolina, visiting and doing business with my cousins. May I join you at your fire?"

"Come out first so that I can see you," ordered Robert.

The man stepped out from behind one of the pine trees, barely twenty feet from their fire. Robert was amazed that he had approached so closely without being detected. He was clearly an Indian, though you could not tell entirely by his clothing. His skin was a deep rust color and darkly tanned. His nose was broad and his face smooth. He wore buckskin breeches and leggings and pucker-toed moccasins. A loose-fitting white collared shirt hung untucked over the top of his breeches. The shirt was open at the collar, exposing his dark bronze and hairless chest. Most of his hair was shaved except for a small tuft on the very back of his head, just below the crown. A thin leather string secured three owl feathers that were protruding out of the tiny tuft of hair.

The man had a tomahawk and two knives tucked inside a narrow leather belt and he carried an old trade musket. He held the musket uncocked and high in his left hand and his empty right hand was in the air. His kindly-looking face beamed with a broad and disarming smile.

"That's far enough," barked Robert, rising to his feet. "You're armed. Why should I trust you?" Robert was trembling, terrified that an actual Indian stood before him. He had seen a few Indians before, but never out in the wilderness … and never in the dark of night.

"Mr. Hammock, if I intended you any harm, I could have killed you and that oldest boy with the rifle a long time ago."

"How do you know my name?" demanded Robert.

The native chuckled, "Well, I just listened to the entire story of your family heritage from London all the way to Amelia County, Virginia. How could I not know your name?"

Little Joshua burst out laughing. His innocent, contagious laughter swept around the campfire and seemed to disarm the tension of the moment. Even Robert smiled.

Robert glanced at Lewis, who was still holding his rifle. "Put the rifle down, son. It's all right." Lewis cautiously placed the weapon on the ground beside his feet and covered it with his blanket.

Robert issued an invitation to the nighttime visitor, "Sir, please leave your weapons by the tree and come join us by the fire."

"My pleasure," returned the Indian. He leaned his musket against a pine tree and removed his belt, piling his bladed weapons beside the musket.

Robert stood and walked toward the Indian, extending his hand in greeting. The grinning native smiled warmly and shook his hand with a strong grip. Robert noticed that the Indian had a very musky, earthy odor about him. It was not a very pleasant odor, but it was not entirely unpleasant, either. He decided that he would try to ignore it.

The Indian introduced himself, "My name is Wappanakuk. My home is not far, about one more day's walk to the north."

Robert responded, "Wappanakuk, I am honored to meet you. As you already know, I am Robert Hammock. This is my wife Milly and my sons Lewis, Robert, Joshua, and John. The young one is our baby, Nancy. We are going to Georgia to begin a home there."

Wappanakuk nodded, "Many white men are traveling the King's Highway and many other roads and trails to the land of Georgia. I have encountered many more like you."

"So you said that your home is nearby?" inquired Robert.

"Yes, Mr. Hammock. My people are the Waccon. You English often call us Waccamaw. My tribe moved north out of South Carolina and settled here near the Green Swamp many years ago. Over the years we have learned the ways of the English. We mastered agriculture and trade, and we learned how to file claims for land and make farms. We are happy and peaceful here."

"You speak perfect English, Wappanakuk. Where did you learn our language?" inquired Milly.

"Many years ago there were preachers and missionaries who helped us. But we had to learn English in order to trade and prosper. Our encounters with the white man have not always been good for my people. Many of my ancestors perished from the diseases that the white man introduced to our tribe and lands. Many thousands more were taken into slavery. Our tribe is a very small one now, and we are a people of peace. Many of our people are of mixed race." He smiled wryly, "Even I had one grandfather who was an Englishman." He winked at Lewis.

"You mentioned that you would like some food," interrupted Milly.

"Oh, yes, Mrs. Hammock. I have not eaten anything but a few edible plants and unripe berries from the forest since yesterday afternoon. I most definitely would not refuse a meal. And what you have in that pot over there smells very good!"

"Well then, Wappanakuk, I will see what I can do to satisfy that hunger of yours."

Milly moved gracefully to the wagon and retrieved a large wooden soup bowl and a half-loaf of bread. She spooned a generous portion of the stew into the bowl, inserted a pewter spoon, and presented the meal to their new friend.

"Oh, thank you, Mrs. Hammock. You are most generous."

"Not a'tall, Wappanakuk. Would you like some hot tea, as well?"

"Yes, ma'am. That would be wonderful. I have not tasted tea in many days."

"With sugar?" she inquired.

"Is there any other way to enjoy tea?" he responded.

Again, laughter flowed around the campfire.

While their Indian guest feasted on the hot stew and bread, the family peppered him with questions about his people and the area around Green Swamp. Robert wanted to know more about the road toward the south and conditions in South Carolina. Wappanakuk answered every question in between bites of stew and bread. He clearly enjoyed being the center of attention.

Wappanakuk methodically worked his way through two hearty bowls of stew and ate the entire portion of bread that Milly had given him. Afterward he sat stoically, legs crossed, sipping a cup of Milly's steaming hot tea. Robert offered him his tobacco sack.

Wappanakuk sniffed the cloth sack. "That smells wonderful! Do you mind if I get my tomahawk? It is the only pipe that I have with me. I left the small pipe that my grandfather made for me at my home."

"Of course," responded Robert.

Wappanakuk fetched his English pipe tomahawk from beneath the tree and sat back down beside the fire. He packed the shiny metal bowl with the fragrant tobacco. Robert pulled a fresh coal out of the fire with his pipe tongs and handed it to the Indian. He pressed the glowing coal down into the tobacco and sucked methodically, drawing the heat down into the bowl and exhaling delicious puffs of blue-white smoke.

Wappanakuk closed his eyes and sighed. "Mr. Hammock, that is simply delicious. It must be Virginia tobacco."

Robert grinned. "Is there any other way to enjoy a pipe?"

Wappanakuk threw back his head and laughed enthusiastically.

Robert, Jr., felt a sudden flash of boldness and asked the Indian a question. "Can you tell us a story, Wappanakuk? We like Papa's stories, but we've heard them all so many times."

The Indian responded, "Would you like to hear a story about my people ... the Waccon people ... and our ancestral home?"

"Oh, yes!" responded the children.

The Indian took a gigantic puff from the tomahawk pipe and began his tale, "Well, many thousands of years ago my people lived in this land in great numbers. They were like the stars in the sky! My ancestors were people of the rivers, going great distances for many days in their long canoes. They traveled to many places to the south and west, even to the great pointed mountains!

"Their home was a large village near here. That village had a beautiful garden that was full of flowers from all of the places where the warriors had traveled. They brought back these beautiful plants and placed them in the garden to honor themselves and all of their adventures in their canoes. The women of the village spent many hours each day tending the garden. Many animals lived there, as well. It was a perfect place.

"But over time the people became arrogant and full of themselves. They spent so much time honoring their achievements and their accomplishments that they forgot to honor their great Creator. And so the Creator decided that he must punish his children.

"One night a strange light filled the sky to the southwest. And as each day passed into night the light grew brighter and brighter. It was a great ball of fire in the sky with a long tail that followed it, and it soon filled the skies with its brilliance. It shined like another sun in the nighttime.

"Finally, after many days, the great ball of fire struck the garden and the village, destroying them both. It slammed into the ground and penetrated deep into the earth. The impact of this great fireball made the ground ripple in waves like the water so that no man nor beast could stand. There was a great wave of fire that extended out for many miles from the place where the fireball landed, consuming the forests and animals. Everything was charred black with fires of destruction.

"But at the center, in the place where the great ball of fire with the flaming, smoking tail struck the earth, there remained a giant, deep hole. And it drew into it the waters of all the nearby rivers and swamps. These waters cooled the great fire deep in the earth and then the waters turned the most amazing, deep green-blue color that your mind could ever imagine. That place is now Lake Waccamaw. Its waters are pure and sweet and clear. It is this lake that marks the homeland of my people.

"We have vowed that we will never again forget the Creator. So my people live in peace with the Holy One. My lodge sits in peace beside the waters of this beautiful, blue lake. And my people, the Waccon people, are now known as the 'People of the Falling Star.'"

Adults and children alike sat breathless, clinging to

every word of the great story of the meteor and the lake. They wanted and expected more.

Wappanakuk made a comical face and shrugged. "That is it, my friends. That is my entire story!"

The members of the Hammock family cheered and clapped with glee.

Lewis chirped, "You need to learn some new stories like that one, Papa!"

Robert nodded and smiled. "I'm sure that we'll write many new stories of our own in Georgia someday. And just think about our memories from this night! For the rest of our lives we'll remember and tell one another and our children and grandchildren about the night that Wappanakuk of the Waccon people stepped out of the darkness and joined us at our fire during our great journey."

Milly rose from her spot near the fire. "Children, it is time that we call an end to our evening. We have a long day of travel ahead of us tomorrow. Come, let us prepare for bed."

In that moment the loud click of a flintlock being brought to full cock echoed in the darkness that lurked beyond the reach of their campfire. It was followed by two other similar clicks.

A voice echoed from that darkness. "Woo-wee! That was some good story!"

Robert began to reach for his pistol but a gruff voice from beyond the pines interrupted the attempt. "Just keep on reaching if you're ready to die tonight, fine sir! I have my musket aimed straight at your belly. Now get those hands up in the air and kick that pistol away from you … nice and slow."

CHAPTER FIVE
TAROWA YETASHTA

Robert slowly raised his hands. As he did so he stole a glance at his wife and children. Fear filled their eyes. Robert experienced a strange combination of heartbreak and terror. He was frightened for his family. He spoke with a trembling voice, "There's no need for violence. You can take whatever you want. Just be quick about it and leave us in peace."

Three rough, grimy men stepped out of the darkness. They all wore threadbare, nasty clothes and stained floppy hats. They each carried rusty muskets and had pistols tucked into their hunting belts.

The man who stood in the center responded angrily, "You aren't in a position to be making any conditions, sir! We are in charge here, and I reckon we'll help ourselves to whatever we want."

The man to his right swung his musket toward Wappanakuk. "Now ain't this somethin', Tom? This here bunch has done gone and got themselves a pet Injun!" The man looked at Robert. "Reckon he does any tricks?"

Robert did not respond. Neither did Wappanakuk, who kept his hands in the air and stared glossy-eyed into the fire. His face showed no emotion and he completely ignored the three bandits.

The taunting man sprinted forward and jabbed the barrel of his musket in the Indian's back and screeched, "I said, does your Injun do any tricks? Maybe he can do us a little war dance or call up some rain? We ain't had a good rain in quite a spell."

Again there was no response.

"Shut up, Shad," commanded the man in the middle ... the one called Tom. He was obviously the leader of the group. "We aren't here to play, we're here to take. Less talking and more taking. Now here's what's going to happen, folks You children are going to stay right where you are while the mister moves over by the big chief. Go on, mister fancy man. Snuggle up against that Injun friend of yours."

Robert obeyed, his hands high in the air.

The robber grinned with satisfaction. "Good. That's good. Keep doing what you're told and you just might see daylight in the morning. Now Shad, you keep an eye on these nice folks by the fire. Ed, you take a look-see in that wagon and find out what manner of good stuff it's got in it."

The filthy man reached over and whipped Milly's bonnet off of her head and grabbed a handful of her long hair, yanking her to her feet. Milly screamed in horror and pain.

Robert started to jump to his feet to protect his wife, but the highwayman standing behind him yanked his pistol from his belt and clubbed him over the head with it. It was a horrible blow. Robert went limp and passed out, almost landing in the fire. Wappanakuk reached over quickly and pulled him away from the coals.

"Now ain't that a good Injun?" remarked the assailant who had struck Robert.

"Good work, Shad," said the leader. "Ed, go check the wagon."

45

Ed turned around and took three steps toward the rig. He stuck his face into the rear opening in the canvas.

He screamed, "Hey! There's somebody in —"

He never finished his sentence. Inside the wagon there was a deafening explosion and brilliant flash of light. Someone had fired a pistol. Ed spun around, clutching at a bullet wound in his chest, and collapsed motionless in the dirt.

"What in the world?" exclaimed the man called Shad. He spun around and was lifting his musket to fire into the wagon. Just at that moment the canvas flap flew open and a single dark arm and shiny brown face emerged into the light of the campfire. And at the end of that arm was a pistol.

It was Frank.

He instantly pulled the trigger on the pistol, the spring releasing the hammer and slamming the flint forward into the frizzen. The pistol barked and sent its lead ball flying at the startled man. It struck him solidly in the center of his chest, knocking him off of his feet. The man landed flat on his back with a thud. He did not move.

The moment that Frank shot the second robber Wappanakuk jumped to his feet and lunged toward the leader ... the man who held Milly in a headlock. The Indian screamed a blood-curdling battle cry as he attacked. The bandit threw Milly aside and reached for the pistol in his belt, but his hand never touched the wood. Wappanakuk's pipe tomahawk was already airborne, leaving a trail of smoke in the air from the smoldering tobacco in its bowl. It impacted with a gigantic thump into the man's chest. He collapsed onto the ground.

Another weapon discharged somewhere in the darkness. There was a fourth attacker who had remained hidden in the trees. The secret bandit had fired at Wappanakuk. A scream of frustration pierced the night as the man came running into the firelight with a pistol in his hand. He intended to shoot Wappanakuk. But before he could pull back the cock on his pistol another shot rang out. The man spun wildly to his left and screamed as a lead ball impacted his ribcage just below his heart. He collapsed motionless near the campfire.

That final shot was fired by Lewis Hammock. As the combat had raged around him, he reached beneath the blanket at his feet and retrieved his hunting rifle just as the fourth man fired his errant shot at Wappanakuk. Lewis had instinctively cocked and fired and brought down the last attacker.

The campsite was suddenly quiet. The smoke of rifle and pistol fire hung in a dull haze. Milly wept in shock.

Frank walked over to her and placed a hand on her shoulder. "Miss Milly, why don't you take the children around on the other side of the wagon?"

She kept staring and did not move.

Frank yelled rather loudly, "Miss Milly!"

Frank's loud voice broke through the fog of her confusion. She nodded and gathered her younger children and took them around the wagon. Robert Hammock, still unconscious from the blow to his head, had missed the entire fight.

Wappanakuk was staring at Frank. Lewis saw a look of confusion on the Indian's face. He said, "Wappanakuk, this is my big brother, Frank. He got hurt a few days ago and was sleeping in the wagon."

An even deeper look of confusion showed on Wappanakuk's face. Frank just grinned as he reloaded the pistol in his hand.

The sun was already steaming hot, and it was only mid-morning. Everyone was exhausted. No one had been able to sleep after the horrible events of the night before. The boys worked together to pack all of the family belongings back into the wagon. Finally, it was time for the Hammock family to depart.

Robert mounted his horse and then leaned over the pommel of his saddle to shake Wappanakuk's hand. He spoke earnestly, "My friend, I cannot thank you enough for what you did for my family."

Wappanakuk pumped his hand vigorously. "Robert, I am just glad that we defeated those horrible bandits, and that they will never harm another traveler on this highway. It was a great battle and a great victory over our enemies!"

He nodded toward Frank. "But let it be remembered that it was Frank who truly saved us all. I fear that we would all be dead had he not been so handy with a pistol."

Frank, who was checking the straps on the wagon team, smiled and tipped his hat to the Indian.

Robert spoke with deep emotion, "Wappanakuk, I want you to know that you are welcome in my home and beside my fire at any time. If you ever wander down Georgia way, please seek us out and come for a visit."

"I will, Robert. I promise. But you must be careful down there in Georgia. You will be living on the border of the Creek lands. You must remain alert!"

"I know, Wappanakuk. I will always be on the lookout."

"I will think often of you and your family. You are fine people. But I fear deeply for you all in the coming days. I hear many rumors that the white men may soon go to war with one another in order to cast off the government of the English. There will be no escaping such a war anywhere in the colonies. It will also affect Georgia, as well. And like in the great war between the English and the French, it will be most difficult on the people native to this land."

"I hope that you are wrong, Wappanakuk. I certainly think that it is foolish to go to war with England. Perhaps such a war will not find its way to the frontiers of Georgia. I can always hope."

"Indeed you can, my friend," responded the gentle native.

Wappanakuk turned and walked toward Lewis, who stood waiting beside the wagon. He bowed gently at the waist and extended his hand to the boy.

"Lewis, I will forever owe you a debt of life and blood. You saved my life … that is certain. That last man would have killed me had it not been for your quick reaction and skillful shot. You will always be my brother and my friend."

Lewis's face flushed crimson with a mixture of pride and embarrassment. He removed his cocked hat with his free hand and responded sheepishly, "Thank you, Wappanakuk. You are most kind."

The Indian held onto the boy's hand and fixed his gaze deep into Lewis's eyes. "I need you to hear me, Lewis, and understand. I am not speaking lightly. I mean every word that I say, from the depths of my heart. This is very important. My life has been made longer because of you. I have more days to live and enjoy this beautiful world because of you, and I want to give you some things to honor your gift to me. First, I want to give you something very personal."

Wappanakuk reached around the back of his neck and lifted over his head a necklace of brilliant blue and green beads suspended on a thick thread. He placed the necklace around Lewis's neck.

"Lewis, these beads represent my heritage and family. Each bead tells a very important part of the story of my people. I want you to keep them so that you will always remember me."

"Thank you, Wappanakuk. I will wear them for the rest of my life."

"This, too, is yours." Wappanakuk placed a tomahawk in his hand. "This is a valuable tomahawk of the Cherokee people. It is a beautiful piece of art, yet it is also a powerful weapon. This tomahawk was carried by the man that you defeated in battle. And this is the hunting knife that he carried. By right of victory they are both yours. I urge you to carry them every day as you defend and help care for your family."

Lewis received the weapons and dutifully tucked them inside his leather waist belt.

"And I want to give you something else, Lewis. Since you are now my blood brother, I want to bestow upon you a Waccon name that is worthy of my family. From now on, to me and among the Waccon people, you will be known as Tarowa Yetashta."

Lewis was on the verge of crying. "What does that mean?" he asked.

"It means, 'Little Warrior.' And I know that you will live up to that name for all of the days of your life. You will always be a great warrior and defender of your family and your home. Now, go in peace and prosperity, Tarowa Yetashta."

Lewis threw his arms around the Indian and hugged him tightly. Wappanakuk patted the boy's shoulder and laughed with joy.

"Come along, Lewis," encouraged Robert. "Our friend must return to his home today, and we must go in search of a new home."

Lewis jumped energetically onto his horse and eased up alongside his father. Frank, obviously much better after several days of recuperation, was back in his seat on the wagon and prepared to drive the team.

Wappanakuk bent over and picked up his bundle of weapons, pulling the leather strap over his head and crossing it across his chest and left shoulder. He waved and said, "I wish peace and safe journey for the Hammock family of Georgia."

And with that brief salute Wappanakuk turned and began to walk slowly and deliberately to the northwest.

Robert faced Lewis and Frank. "Let's go, boys. No need to rush today. Just keep a steady pace. And everyone drink plenty of water. It looks like it's going to be a scorcher."

The Hammock clan guided their animals back onto the road and headed southwest, hoping to put some miles between themselves and the horror of the previous night.

CHAPTER SIX
ON TO GEORGIA!

Several days later the Hammocks reached Charlestown in South Carolina. It was the largest city in South Carolina, complete with a huge harbor and port. People of all imaginable races and nationalities walked the streets pursuing their trades and businesses. There were hundreds of street vendors hawking their wares. Little boys sold newspapers on street corners. The air had a thick and almost overwhelming smell of cook fires and stinky fish. The Hammock children poked their heads out of various holes in the wagon to observe the carnival of humanity in the streets.

Robert's voice broke the colorful city's hold on their eyes and thoughts. "Let's board these horses for the night, do a little business, and find us a bed and a hot bath."

"A hot bath!" exclaimed Milly. "That will be magnificent!"

After securing a livery to shelter their horses and wagon and finding suitable lodging for the night in a decent boarding house, the family went in search of supplies. Robert purchased a sack of dried beans and a large sack of rice, a staple in the local South Carolina diet. He also replenished their supply of tea, salt, and sugar. A small keg of salted pork and a similar keg of salted beef finished their supply order. They hauled all of the goods back to the wagon and stowed them safely beneath their canvas cover.

They quickly sought out a bath house and laundry so that they could all have a proper wash and a thorough cleaning of their clothes. Afterwards they located a nice tavern on the same street as their lodging and enjoyed a tasty meal of roasted beef with potatoes and carrots accompanied by copious quantities of steaming, delicious bread.

The remainder of their evening in Charlestown was uneventful … very different from their experiences in the North Carolina city of New Bern. Sleep came very easily that night in the comfort of warm feather beds.

Robert roused the family and prepared them for travel shortly before sunrise the next morning. He was eager to get out of the overcrowded city. Frank and Lewis fetched the horses and rig from the livery and tied them up in front of the boarding house. The boys loaded the family's personal boxes and bags into the wagon. As the daylight overcame the darkness of the dawn they were just preparing to mount up and continue southward when they heard a loud voice calling from somewhere down the street.

"Robert Hammock!"

Robert, somewhat confused, looked around and tried to identify a familiar face in the growing early morning crowd, but he saw none. Thinking it a fluke, he turned his attention back toward the buckles on his saddle. Then he heard it again.

"Hello there! Robert Hammock of Georgia!"

Lewis shouted, "Look, Papa! It's Mr. Chandler!"

Robert spun around and at last saw the familiar of Christopher Chandler.

"Chris!" Robert exclaimed. "I thought you folks would already be in Savannah by now!"

The young fellow ran toward Robert. He shook Robert's hand enthusiastically and smiled with pleasure at having encountered the Hammock family again.

"Well, Robert, we had a setback. The other families moved on four days ago. They headed straight for Augusta. But we had to stay behind."

Milly interrupted the conversation. "What happened, Mr. Chandler? Is dear Esther all right?"

Chris removed his hat and nodded courteously at Milly. "Ma'am, she's fine in body, but she's truly suffering in her soul." The young man's chin dropped to his chest and his countenance fell. A tear formed in his right eye, swelled, and then ran down his cheek.

Milly inquired further, "Chris, what's wrong?"

"It's our baby, Agnes."

"Is the child ill? I have some medicine. We can tend to her right now!" Milly rose to climb over the wagon seat and fetch the medicine bag from its place in the wagon.

"It's no use, Miss Milly. Our baby is gone. She came down with a fever right about the time we got into South Carolina. We nursed her as best we could until we got to Charlestown. She held on for a bit, but it was just too much for her tiny body. She passed away the day before yesterday." The young man was heartbroken.

"Oh, Chris, I am so very sorry!" Milly climbed down from the wagon and walked to the man, taking gentle hold of his arm. "You must take me to Esther right now. I will help tend to her."

Christopher shook his head. "I don't want to trouble you good folks. You're all set to finish this last leg of the journey to Georgia."

Robert spoke up, "We can minister to your wife along the way, Chris. Milly can ride with her in your wagon. Our little ones are big enough to take care of themselves. We'll manage just fine. We have just another three days or so to Savannah. Surely Milly can help restore her mind and spirit in three days. Are you prepared to leave now?"

"Yes, sir. I have all of our belongings and provisions loaded and ready. I'll just need to fetch the wagon and team and gather the few personal belongings we still have in the boarding house."

"I'll go with you now and help finish your packing and then help get Esther in the wagon," volunteered Milly. "Robert and the kids will wait for us and then we'll all head south together. Isn't that right, Robert?"

"Indeed. We will go ahead and get out of the city. We'll be waiting for you just outside of town on the Charlestown-Savannah Trail. I promise that we'll be right on the shoulder of the road. You won't miss us."

Chris said, "I don't know how I can ever repay you folks."

Robert shook his hand firmly. "You can repay me by walking into the Savannah land office with me and claiming a land grant as my neighbor." Robert smiled warmly.

Chris smiled back. "I can do that, Robert."

"Good. Now go get your bride and let's get rolling toward our new homes. Time's a wasting! I hear Georgia calling!"

"Yes, sir. I'll see you in a bit." The young man offered Milly his arm in a most gentlemanly manner and escorted her up the street toward his boarding house.

Robert watched them disappear around the corner and then turned to Frank and Lewis. "Boys, there's too many people in this stinky city. Let's get out of town and wait out in the countryside where it's more peaceful."

"Amen to that!" exclaimed Frank. Lewis punched him in the shoulder and giggled.

Robert and Lewis mounted their horses and Frank hopped up onto the seat of the wagon. Moments later they were threading their way through the already bustling streets of the city. A few blocks away they saw a sign marked "Savannah." It had a large arrow that pointed down a wide stretch of road to the southwest.

"There it is, boys ... the Charlestown-Savannah Trail. That's our road to Georgia."

They turned their horses in the direction indicated by the sign, heading due west. It took a half-hour to get all the way clear of the civilization of town. Robert guided his horse to a large oak tree near the roadway as Lewis and Frank followed suit. They waited and rested in the shade. The kids all clamored out of the wagon and passed the time playing in the adjoining meadow.

Their wait was brief. Roughly an hour later they saw another wagon headed in their direction. Christopher Chandler sat in the seat. He waved at the Hammocks.

"Let's go, boys. We've dawdled long enough. Let's just pull out in front of them and roll on. We can visit later," Robert declared.

So the convoy was on the move. Once again the steady, familiar routine of travel set in. They traveled hard by day and made camp shortly before dark each evening. The countryside of South Carolina was quiet and peaceful. It took a few days, but Esther's spirits did seem to get better. Everyone's spirits improved the closer they came to Georgia.

It was five days later when Lewis spotted the sign that they had been waiting for. A rough-cut sign nailed to a fencepost said, "Savannah - 10 miles."

"There it is!" exclaimed Lewis. "We're almost to Georgia! We're almost home!"

Robert nodded. "Yes, indeed. We would be hard-pressed to make it before sundown today, but we'll definitely cross the river before noon tomorrow."

The nearness of their destination breathed fresh life into the weary travelers. They drove on. Recent rains left several deep muddy spots that were very difficult to cross.

The road conditions slowed them down somewhat, but they still managed another six or seven miles before time to camp. Everyone was too excited to sleep that night, knowing that they would be in Georgia the following day. But the sleep of exhaustion finally overwhelmed their excitement.

Dawn came quickly, and both families were fed and on the move less than an hour after the sunrise. They covered the final stretch with ease and pulled up to the ferry crossing on the northern bank of the river. They paid their fare and less than an hour later both wagons and all riders were safely across into Georgia.

Savannah was a vibrant, bustling little city. Several small ships were anchored in the channel of the river. Small cargo boats were busy shuttling goods back and forth between the wharves and the ships. The docks and warehouses were stacked high with boxes and sacks. Dozens of men labored along the waterfront in the commerce and trade of the Georgia colony.

Chris pulled his wagon alongside the Hammock rig. Robert and Lewis dismounted and walked between the teams to join in a convoy conference.

"Welcome to Georgia. Finally!" shouted Robert.

Everyone smiled. The women seemed joyful ... and relieved. Even the small children were giddy.

"What now?" asked Chris. "Where do we go? How do we get our land?"

"Well, I suppose we need to go in search of the colonial land office and file our land claim with the King's representative. It should be easy enough to find," responded Robert.

A half-hour later the weary travelers pulled up in front of a lovely two-story red brick building. A sign hung over the front door, stating, "*Hon. Walter Wickersham, Trustee - Georgia Colony Land Office.*"

"This is the place," proclaimed Robert. "Chris and I will go inside and take care of business. Frank, you keep watch over the wagons. Come inside and get me if there's any trouble."

"I will, sir," Frank responded obediently.

"Lewis, you come with me. I want you to see how all of this land business works. You'll be in charge of the family business one day."

"Yes, Papa."

The two men and Lewis climbed the three steps to the porch stoop and opened the front door. A bell mounted over the door notified anyone inside of their arrival. They heard heavy footsteps emanating from the stairway to the second floor. Moments later a rather portly gentleman in a lavishly-patterned and colorful formal coat and bright purple stockings and breeches bounded onto the oak floor at the bottom of the stairs. The floor strained and creaked ever-so-slightly upon his arrival. The man had a jolly look about him. His cheeks were flushed red and he was smiling broadly.

He greeted them with a voice thickened by an accent native of England, "Ahh … good day to you, gentlemen! I am Walter Wickersham, serving as one of the King's trustees in the allotment of lands in His Majesty's Georgia colony."

"God save the King!" stated Robert and Christopher simultaneously.

The jolly man smiled even more broadly, "Yes, indeed! God save the King! Now to what do I owe the pleasure of your visit on this beautiful Georgia morning?"

"Mr. Wickersham, I am Robert Hammock, formerly of Virginia. This is Christopher Chandler, also formerly of Virginia."

"Wonderful! And who is this little fellow?" He offered a handshake to Lewis.

"I'm Lewis Hammock, Sir, the oldest son of Robert Hammock."

The English gentleman laughed warmly. "So, you are, eh? Well, aren't you a well-spoken lad? It is a pleasure to meet you Squire Hammock." He directed his attention at the grown men. "Now, what brings you to my office today?"

Robert responded, "We are here to file for claims on the frontier. We and our families wish to settle and make a life in Georgia."

"Oh, good show! Good show, indeed! Families, you say? We need good, solid farming families to help us tame these wild lands on the frontier." Wickersham walked over to them and shook their hands vigorously. "And when will your families be joining you?"

"Oh, they're already here, sir. They're all waiting in our wagons outside," responded Chris.

"Oh, you brought your families! Splendid! How delightful! I trust that you had a safe and uneventful journey."

"Not quite," answered Robert. "We came upon a little trouble in North Carolina. But it was nothing that we couldn't handle. We made the journey in a little over three weeks." Robert decided not to go into any detail about their trouble with the British soldiers in New Bern.

"Well, I don't doubt that North Carolina gave you some trouble. There's a rebellious mood in that colony." Wickersham paused and looked carefully into the eyes of the men standing before him. "If I may be so bold, gentlemen ... procedure requires that I must ask you ... where do your political allegiances lie?"

"To King and country, sir," responded Robert.

"To King and country," affirmed Chris.

"Excellent! Now let's get down to business."

Chris interrupted him, "Sir, I've heard there have been some Indian troubles. Is the land safe enough for us to settle?"

"Oh, quite. In fact, the place where I will allocate your lands will be some of the most beautiful and peaceful lands in that region. I promise you. I plan to reward you for your bravery and your pioneer spirit. Gentlemen, I cannot describe to you how beautiful this place is. Gently rolling hills, rich soil, plenty of water. Indeed, Governor Wright has declared that it looks exactly like many parts of England, itself! A paradise! Now ... let's do some paperwork and get you gentlemen on your way to your new homes."

He handed them a slip of paper. "Please list the names and ages of each person in your household."

Lewis watched intently as Robert read and then wrote numbers down on the paper.

"Why does he need these numbers, Papa?"

"Son, he needs them to calculate how much land we are entitled to in our claims."

"Oh. So the more people you have, the more land you get?"

"Yes, son. That's it, exactly."

A few minutes later Mr. Wickersham took their papers, retrieved his pen, and performed a simple calculation. "Mr. Hammock, according to the statutes governing land claims, you are entitled to one hundred acres for yourself, plus an additional fifty acres for each member of your household, including slaves. I shall issue a land claim for you today in the amount of four hundred acres."

"Four hundred acres?" exclaimed Robert.

The round-faced man smiled. "Is there a problem, Mr. Hammock?"

"No, sir. No problem, at all. I had no idea it would be so much."

"There is plenty of land available, sir, and His Majesty intends to reward those with the courage to claim it and tame it. Now, Mr. Chandler, your allotment today is one hundred and fifty acres of beautiful Georgia land."

"Thank you, sir. I am most grateful," Chris responded.

"Very well. Now! Allow me to show you the location of your claims."

Wickersham made his way to a large map posted on the office wall.

"Your lands will be located here," he pointed to a spot on the map. "I will assign you both lands along Reedy Creek. You will undoubtedly love this spot! It is only a few miles from Wrightsborough, a quaint village founded by several dozen Quaker families who settled the region in 1767. They are good, solid, peace-loving folk. And the best part is that the Creeks respect them and value them as neighbors. They will be good allies for you as you establish a home."

"That sounds wonderful to me, sir," remarked Robert. "I don't know much about the Quakers, but I hear that they are good neighbors."

"Jolly good, then. Now if you gentlemen can give me two hours to prepare the necessary documents and draw up the claims, I will have your matter settled and you can be on your way. The noon hour is approaching, so perhaps you can enjoy tea here in our fair city as you wait."

"Than sounds wonderful, sir. How long is the journey?" asked Chris.

"Oh, it is still quite the distance, I'm afraid. You will need provisions for an additional four days of travel. It may take a bit more, or a bit less. But with families and wagons, I would plan for at least four days, perhaps five to be safe. I dare say you can purchase any supplies that you need here in Savannah. Now, if you will give me some time to prepare the documents, I will have you gentlemen on your way in two hours."

Shortly after noon the Hammock and Chandler wagons were bouncing northwest along the wagon road toward Augusta ... toward their new lives on the Georgia frontier.

Part II

1776 - Frontier Battles

CHAPTER SEVEN
A DECLARATION OF INDEPENDENCE

It was mid-August, 1776. There had been almost no rain in over a week, and the ground was beginning to look parched. Robert scanned the skies, hoping and praying for a late afternoon shower or storm to wet the thirsty field. He saw a thin wisp of dust making its way toward him from the house. Someone was approaching the cornfield from the cabin, obviously running on the well-worn and dusty footpath.

His friend and farming partner, Chris Chandler, pointed toward the growing dust cloud. "Here comes the Hammock version of the dinner bell. I wonder which little Hammock it will be today."

Soon a handsome little fellow wearing a floppy straw hat came into view from behind the corner of the waist-high corn. It was nine-year-old Joshua Hammock.

"Papa! Mr. Chandler! Mama says it's time for supper, and that nobody gets to eat until you both come in from the field!"

"We'll be right along, Joshua. Tell your mother to be patient."

The boy smiled and waved and then spun around, darting back in the direction from which he had come. His short queue flopped haphazardly as he ran. Robert chuckled as he watched the little wave of dust dancing upward above the corn, marking the child's progress back toward the cabin.

Robert and Chris both sighed deep breaths of satisfaction and simultaneously crossed their arms, surveying the crop that grew lush and tall in the field before them. Though it needed a good drink of water, it was still a five acre field of healthy-looking corn. It would be an excellent food and cash crop in the fall. Corn was a difficult crop to tend, but the Hammocks had plenty of young laborers to help chop and beat back the forest and weeds that steadily attempted to reclaim the cleared land.

The family also had a garden. It was a huge garden. Milly and the children had almost an entire acre of every imaginable vegetable and herb planted near the Hammock cabin. They worked, chopped, weeded, and watered the precious food source every single day. The family had been enjoying the fruits of the garden since the first week of June. But it was just now beginning to yield its true bounty. The hot August weather and warm nights were perfect for high yields and luscious flavor. It was a hundred times better and more productive than any garden that they had ever attempted to grow in Virginia.

But as happy and successful as life seemed for the Hammock family, it had been two difficult, laborious years since their arrival on the frontier. Robert's land claim and that of his neighbor, Chris Chandler, were beautiful and fertile beyond expectation. There was plenty of timber, ample game, and abundant fresh water. Crops seemed to grow with minimal effort. It was the perfect place for pioneer families, once the land was cleared of trees, and as long as hostile Indians left them alone.

Thus far Robert and Chris had enjoyed a state of peace along Reedy Creek. A single cow stolen in the dead of night was their only loss so far. The thief could have either been a white settler or a Creek or Cherokee raider. They would never know.

The two families enjoyed a relatively peaceful first two years on the frontier, but Robert knew that trouble was coming. A war had erupted in the Colonies. There was open rebellion against England, having started in Massachusetts and then spread to New York and New Jersey and beyond. Men in the Americas wanted more self-governance and less oppressive taxes. Robert tended to agree with their politics, but thus far he was not pleased with their methods. He wanted no part of a war with England.

Recently the rebellion had made its way into Georgia. There was some fighting along the coast. There had also been a particularly violent event in nearby Augusta in August of 1775. A gentleman planter and well-known Loyalist by the name of Thomas Brown was taken hostage by a mob stirred up by the Sons of Liberty. The man was tied to a stake and then burned, scalped, tarred, and feathered. Unbelievably, he survived all of his wounds. Everyone knew that Thomas Brown was a determined and powerful man. He would, no doubt, one day seek his vengeance upon his enemies in Augusta.

It seemed that Georgia, the youngest and most "British" of all the thirteen Colonies, would soon become caught up in the violence of Revolution.

Robert Hammock had no special love for the British. Most of his loyalties vanished after Frank's violent encounter with the Redcoats in New Bern, North Carolina. The arrogant, condescending remarks of the British officer toward colonial citizens pretty much solidified Robert's sentiments toward independence in the Americas. But as he pondered the growing war, and the possibility of bloodshed in Georgia, he wondered if there might be more peaceful methods to achieve the same goal.

Chris tapped Robert on the shoulder, jarring him from

the solitude of this thoughts. "The women are waiting, Robert. We'd best be getting along, or there may be consequences." Chris winked at his friend.

The two men walked briskly toward the Hammock home, the place where both households regularly ate their meals. Minutes later they emerged from beneath the shade of the tall walnut tree that stood between the cornfield and the cabin. Milly had just stepped inside the cabin. Esther stood beside the table, keeping watch over the hungry, waiting children.

Robert looked around the table and noticed some conspicuous absences. "Where are Lewis and Frank? I haven't seen either of them all day."

Esther replied, "Milly sent them over to Wrightsborough just after breakfast. We need a few supplies."

"The boys should be back any minute, I suspect," Milly retorted as she stepped out of the cabin. "They were on horseback. But there's nothing to stop us from going ahead and enjoying our supper. Robert, Jr., you will say grace."

Little Robert dutifully stood up from his seat at the table and offered the prayer for the meal. The moment that his, "Amen," departed his lips the two tables full of hungry pioneers attacked the bountiful meal with gusto. They ravaged the delicious food. A half-hour later they sat around the table enjoying tea and small servings of bread pudding. Robert and Chris smoked their pipes.

Robert kept glancing down the narrow path toward Wrightsborough. He was beginning to get worried about the boys. It would be dark soon.

Lewis loved going to the town of Wrightsborough. There were so many things to see and do. Mr. Schwarz's general store was a wonderland of smells and flavors. The old German always managed to have a large stock of colorful and exotic candies and sweets. He loved to bless the local children with small gifts of the flavorful treats.

But there was obviously something more than sweet treats drawing a crowd to Schwarz's store today. There were almost a hundred people crowded around the front of the small building. Lewis noticed a handsome gentleman wearing the dark blue, buff-trimmed coat of the Continental Army standing at the top of the steps. He held a large piece of yellow parchment in his hand.

Frank and Lewis tied their horses to a small tree near the store and made their way quickly to join the crowd.

Lewis saw a friend from town, Micah Foley, sitting on the back of a wagon. He and Frank walked over to the boy.

"Hey, Micah! Why the crowd? Why is everyone so excited?"

"Hello, Lewis ... hey there, Frank," the boy responded. "I'm not really sure. That soldier is from somewhere up north. I think someone said he was from Philadelphia. He's supposed to have a message from the Continental Congress that they've been reading in towns all up and down the coast. He's about to start reading it for us here in just a bit."

"I've never seen a Continental Army uniform before," commented Frank.

"Me, neither," responded Micah. "Kind of spiffy, ain't he? Especially with that pretty curled-up hair and queue. He's a honest-to-goodness gentleman, I reckon."

Lewis and Frank chuckled.

"Look!" said Micah. "I think he's about to start."

The soldier stepped forward onto the top step that led up to the front door of the general store. He tugged at his silk necktie and cleared his throat.

"Ladies and gentlemen! If I may have your attention! I am Lieutenant Horace Allred of the First Pennsylvania

Regiment of the Continental Army. I have been dispatched to Georgia to read the following statement in as many communities and settlements as possible. I urge you to listen carefully to the following proclamation approved in Congress and signed by the representatives of Georgia."

The officer held up the paper and began to read:

IN CONGRESS, July 4, 1776.
The unanimous Declaration of the thirteen United States of America,

When in the Course of human events, it becomes necessary for one people to dissolve the political bands which have connected them with another, and to assume among the powers of the earth, the separate and equal station to which the Laws of Nature and of Nature's God entitle them, a decent respect to the opinions of mankind requires that they should declare the causes which impel them to the separation.

We hold these truths to be self-evident, that all men are created equal, that they are endowed by their Creator with certain unalienable Rights, that among these are Life, Liberty and the pursuit of Happiness.--That to secure these rights, Governments are instituted among Men, deriving their just powers from the consent of the governed, --That whenever any Form of Government becomes destructive of these ends, it is the Right of the People to alter or to abolish it, and to institute new Government, laying its foundation on such principles and organizing its powers in such form, as to them shall seem most likely to effect their Safety and Happiness. Prudence, indeed, will dictate that Governments long established should not be changed for light and transient causes; and accordingly all experience hath shewn, that mankind are more disposed to suffer, while evils are sufferable, than to right themselves by abolishing the forms to which they are accustomed.

But when a long train of abuses and usurpations, pursuing invariably the same Object evinces a design to reduce them under absolute Despotism, it is their right, it is their duty, to throw off such Government, and to provide new Guards for their future security.-- Such has been the patient sufferance of these Colonies; and such is now the necessity which constrains them to alter their former Systems of Government. The history of the present King of Great Britain is a history of repeated injuries and usurpations, all having in direct object the establishment of an absolute Tyranny over these States.

Lewis leaned over and whispered to Frank, "What is this all about? What are states? And what in tarnation are 'usurpations?'"

"Shh," Frank responded. "I'm trying to listen. This is important."

Over the next several minutes the Continental officer read off a long and disturbing list of all of the offenses committed by the British against the people of the Americas. Some of the people at the gathering shouted and shook their fists as each charge against Great Britain was listed. The crowd grew angrier and angrier as each statement was read. Finally, the officer reached the climax of his presentation.

We, therefore, the Representatives of the United States of America, in General Congress, Assembled, appealing to the Supreme Judge of the world for the rectitude of our intentions, do, in the Name, and by Authority of the good People of these Colonies, solemnly publish and declare, That these United Colonies are, and of Right ought to be Free and Independent States; that they are Absolved from all Allegiance to the British Crown, and that all political connection between them and the State of Great Britain, is and ought to be totally dissolved; and that as Free and Independent States, they have full Power to levy War, conclude Peace, contract Alliances, establish Commerce, and to do all other Acts and Things which Independent States may of right do. And for the support of this Declaration, with a firm reliance on the protection of divine Providence, we mutually pledge to each other our Lives, our Fortunes and our sacred Honor.

The entire crowd stood and stared in absolute silence. Lewis still did not understand what he had just heard. But, clearly, it was something very important.

"What does that mean?" Micah wondered aloud. "He used too many fancy words."

"It means we just declared to England that we are our very own country," replied Frank.

"How do you think King George will like that?" asked Lewis.

Frank frowned and shook his head. "He won't."

The distant sound of hoofbeats echoed down the road from Wrightsborough.

"Two riders are coming from east," Chris declared. "Sounds like they're riding fast."

Robert stood to his feet and watched the trail in that direction. "It must be Frank and Lewis. They should have returned home from town a long time ago."

Moments later the boys came into view, lying low over the necks of their horses and riding fast. It didn't take them long to reach the cabin.

"Why are you boys riding those horses so hard?" scolded Robert as he looked down the trail. "Were you being chased?"

"No, sir," answered Frank. He removed his cocked hat and wiped his brow with the sleeve of his work shirt. "We have big news and had to get back home with it as fast as we could."

"What news?" asked Chris.

"We live in a new country now!" squeaked Lewis. "The Continental soldier said so!"

Robert gazed at the boy, confused by his statement. He looked to Frank.

Frank nodded. "It's true, sir. We saw the paper and heard a Continental officer read it at Mr. Schwarz's store in Wrightsborough. The Continental Congress has issued a Declaration of Independence from England. They did it on July 4 in Philadelphia. They absolved the states of all allegiance to the British Crown."

"States?" asked Chris.

"That's what we call the colonies now … states. And all of them together are now the United States of America," Lewis answered.

"How can the Continental Congress speak for Georgia like that?" challenged Robert.

"All three of the Georgia delegates to Congress signed the document," Frank answered. "It's a done deal. The Declaration has been read in cities all up and down the coast. We're just the last to hear about it, since we're so far out on the frontier."

A cloud of foreboding silence hung over the group.

Robert took a deep breath and sighed. "Well, that's it, then. Georgia is going to war with England."

"No doubt the Indians will be stirred up, as well," added Chris.

Robert nodded grimly.

CHAPTER EIGHT
AN OLD FRIEND

The Indian raids along the Georgia frontier began on the last day of September. These raids were more than just the usual efforts to harass settlers and steal livestock. The Creek Indians, supplied and encouraged by the British, attacked homesteads all along the frontier. They killed men and boys in the fields and murdered families in their beds. Blood flowed on the frontier. The Creeks stole property, burned homes and barns, and took captive the women and children that they did not see fit to kill.

There were reports that white men were among the raiding parties. There were rumors that Redcoats had taken part in some of the atrocities.

Despite the attacks, the Hammocks tried to continue a normal life and take care of their farm. The days were filled with hard work. The evenings were reserved for converting the their home into a defensible fortress against future Indian raids. Since most of the work was indoors, they were able to accomplish the task at night by candlelight.

Their main strategy was digging protective trenches in the cabin floor. The men used shovels and picks to dig a trench just beneath the outer walls of the cabin that was two and a half feet wide and approximately three feet deep. This trench gave the men below-ground access to six firing holes that they cut in the second row of logs in the wall, about one foot above the ground.

The holes were nine inches square, and just large enough to fire a rifle or musket. The longer east and west walls had two firing ports each. The more narrow north and south walls had a single hole. At the location of each firing hole the men dug notches in the ground that went an additional three feet back into the room. These notches made it easy for a shooter to simply step backward and pull his weapon inside for loading, or to allow another shooter to rotate into his place.

The women and children helped complete the project by hauling the freshly dug earth in buckets and pails outside the cabin and piling it up against the first two rows of logs. And there was a lot of dirt. It provided a protective layer that was two feet high and almost a foot thick all around the base of the cabin.

The final interior modification was a central cellar hole for the women, infants, and toddlers. It would provide them all with adequate space to be below ground and out of the line of musket fire. Robert insisted that they dig the pit all the way to six feet in depth. It formed roughly a six foot square, with a narrow stairway descending into one side of the hole. The bottom of what they called, "the pit," contained a small bed and various necessities for the children.

Milly wept as she watched the floor of her cabin disappearing. She wailed, "My house will never be the same again. And that hole in the middle looks like a huge grave!"

"That hole is going to keep us out of our graves," responded Robert. He cupped her face in his hands. "Don't worry, my love. One day soon this will all be over and we will fill in all of these trenches."

Once the pit was in, the men decided that it would be a good idea to connect it to the outer trench along the east and west walls. So they dug an additional three-foot cut in both directions and made the connection. They took the dirt from these final short connecting trenches and scattered it evenly on the roof of the cabin in the hope that it would help prevent the wood shingles from catching fire.

Their final security measure was the addition of two sets of iron brackets on the inside of the door posts. Robert had them forged by the Quaker blacksmith in Wrightsborough. The brackets were nailed securely on each side with eight-inch nails, forming a perfect slot into which the men could drop heavy timbers behind the closed door. These timbers were huge blocking bars that prevented the door from opening inward.

When they were finished the cabin was barely livable. The only practical functions that the dug-out cabin served were for sleeping and defense. They placed narrow sleeping pallets inside all of the trenches, spaced strategically between the firing holes. The one positive aspect of sleeping below ground each night was the pleasant temperature. Everyone was actually amazed at how cool the trenches were. They enjoyed the most comfortable August and September nights of sleep that they had ever known.

Life gradually found its new routine. The Hammocks and Chandlers worked, cooked, ate, and enjoyed what little leisure time they had outdoors. At night they took refuge in their cabin bunker.

Two joyful incidents broke the monotony of farm life in September. Esther gave birth to a son, Daniel, on September 9. Three days later Robert and Milly welcomed Lucy into their large and growing family. Both babies were born at night in the little bed which now rested in the bottom of the "pit" in the center of what was once the cabin floor.

The Indian raids continued all over the Georgia frontier. Amazingly, the Hammock and Chandler families remained untouched by all of the violence.

It was February 11, 1777. Robert, Chris, and Frank were in the barn sharpening the axes and saws at the end of a long work day when the warning bell on the front of the house began to ring loudly. Then a woman screamed.

"That was Esther!" Chris proclaimed.

Then they heard Lewis's shrill voice from the front of the cabin. "Indians!"

The men grabbed their weapons and ran as fast as they could toward the door of the cabin, scooping up and herding little children as they went. They were inside their fortress with the timbers dropped behind the heavy oak door in less than a minute.

Once inside Frank realized that he was still holding the axe that he had been sharpening in the barn. He tossed it in the corner of the trench and grabbed his musket, thrusting it through his assigned firing hole and sighting his weapon toward the south. His heart broke when he heard the Hammock girls weeping in the pit behind him.

"I don't see anything to the west!" Robert exclaimed. "Anybody else see them?"

"There's no movement to the south!" responded Frank.

"North looks clear!" answered Chris.

Lewis didn't answer.

Robert snapped at him, "Lewis! Do you see anything?"

"No sir!"

"Who sounded the alarm?" demanded Robert.

Lewis answered, "I did, Papa."

"What did you see?"

"I saw an Indian, plain as day, walking up the road

from Wrightsborough. He was a red man, for sure. I saw a bald head and feathers sticking out everywhere. When I yelled out I saw him run into the woods."

Robert wanted clarification. "So you just saw one Indian?"

"Yes, sir."

Robert tried to assess the situation. "Well, if there's one there ought to be more. But that sure is a curious direction. I wouldn't expect the Creeks to approach us in the open and from the east. Still, let's keep a sharp eye out. Everyone stay still, watch, and listen. And Milly, get those children to be quiet! I can't hear thunder over their loud whining and wailing! There's not a thing to be crying about ... not yet."

So they waited. The children gradually ceased their crying. Seconds seemed like hours. The men were anxious and shaky. They jumped at the sound of every bird and squirrel that moved outside.

Moments later they heard a voice call from the woods to the east. "Hello in the cabin! Is anyone home?"

The men all looked across the room at one another. All they could see was one another's heads above the tops of the trenches, and their faces displayed the total confusion that each was feeling.

Frank asked, "Mr. Robert, does that voice sound familiar to you?"

Robert shrugged. He walked over to Lewis's position and placed his mouth up to the firing hole. "We're in here! Step out in the open where we can see you! Nice and slow!"

Forty yards from the cabin a lone Indian stepped out from behind a poplar tree. He held his weapon at the ready, but did not strike any kind of threatening pose.

The man called to the house, "I was hoping you folks might help me with some directions. I'm looking for Robert Hammock. Do you know where his place is? The people in Wrightsborough said it was over this way."

Robert mumbled, "He does sound familiar. But how do I know that Indian?"

"And how does he know you?" questioned Chris.

Suddenly Lewis shrieked at the top of his lungs, "It's Wappanakuk! Papa! It's Wappanakuk from North Carolina!"

Quick as a flash, Lewis and Frank jumped out of their trenches, ran to the door, and tossed the security bars from their brackets. They threw open the door and Lewis shot through the opening like a rifle ball. Frank was right behind him.

He yelled with joy, "Wappanakuk! I can't believe you came!"

A look of recognition washed across the Indian's face. He threw back his head and gave an enthusiastic native shout, "Ayeeeee!"

Lewis ran straight to the Waccon warrior, who received him with a warm embrace. Wappanakuk stepped back away from Lewis and gave the boy a thorough examination.

"Tarowa Yetashta, I cannot believe the man that you are becoming! Do you still wear my family's beads?"

Lewis reached inside his shirt and proudly displayed the strand of colorful Waccon beads around his neck.

"I and my family are honored, Tarowa Yetashta. But just look at you! You have grown to be almost as tall as me. How old are you now?"

Lewis held his head high and thrust out his chest proudly, "I am twelve years old, Wappanakuk."

"You are not quite the little warrior anymore. We may have to change your name." He winked at Lewis.

The other family members finally reached the reunion that was ongoing in the clearing beside the cabin.

Robert exclaimed, "Wappanakuk, I simply cannot believe that you are here! Why have you traveled so far?"

"To visit my friends in Georgia, of course." He smiled. "I was growing restless at home, anyway. So I thought that I might go on a journey. I was desiring to see your family and to find out about your life in Georgia. And you have other friends! I do not recognize these faces."

"Wappanakuk, these are our neighbors Christopher and Esther Chandler and their newborn son, Daniel. They are staying with us for a while."

"I am pleased to meet you both," Wappanakuk declared, shaking Chris' hand.

"Wappanakuk, we have heard many stories about you around our evening fires," Chris stated. "It is good to finally meet you."

Wappanakuk grinned and rubbed the heads of the smaller Hammock children. "I barely recognize the little ones. They have grown so much in two years. And I see there are more."

Milly answered, "Yes, we have had two daughters since our arrival. Elizabeth was born soon after we got here and baby Lucy was born in September."

"Ahh, Miss Milly! It is so wonderful to see you. I must say that you are as beautiful as ever!"

Milly blushed and grinned from ear to ear.

"Am I to assume that you are just as good a cook as ever?" the Indian asked.

"Well, we'll just have to see about that later today, won't we?" she teased.

"I definitely hope so," he replied.

Wappanakuk looked directly at Frank, who stood quietly in the rear behind the Hammock children. The Indian gently parted the children and approached him with his hand outstretched. "Frank, it makes my heart dance with joy to see you. You look strong and well."

"I am well, sir."

"I am glad that you are still with the Hammock family."

"They are my family, sir. I will always be with them."

Wappanakuk patted Frank on the shoulder. "They are truly blessed to have you. You are a fine man and an impressive warrior."

Robert spoke up, "Wappanakuk, you gave us quite a scare. Lewis sounded the alarm when he saw you on the road."

Wappanakuk nodded. "I apologize, Robert. But Tarowa Yetashta scared me as well! When I heard the woman scream and then the voice cry, 'Indians!' I ran into in the woods. I thought I had walked into the middle of a bunch of Creek warriors!"

Lewis could not contain his excitement, "Wappanakuk, tell us about your journey! What is happening in North Carolina? Did you encounter any danger?"

"Yes, Wappanakuk, we need news from the world. We do not hear much out here on the edge of civilization," agreed Chris.

The native nodded his understanding. "Well, North Carolina is very different. The people are all very excited about this Declaration of Independence from Philadelphia. They fancy themselves part of a new nation and seem quite excited to be rid of Great Britain. They have formed a new assembly, organized local governments and committees, and sought to discard all things British."

"Did you encounter any difficulty on your way here?" asked Chris.

"Not until I crossed the river into Georgia. The people here seem wary of all Indians. No one bothered me, but many looked upon me with suspicious eyes. I felt as if someone might take a shot at me at any moment. So I have tried to avoid as many people as possible."

"And what about your tribe?" inquired Robert. "Has the war made things different for them?"

"The Waccon people are unaffected by these things, at least for now. We are a very small tribe and not strong militarily. I do not think that anyone, whether British or American, will be approaching us or any other tribal people as allies or partners any time soon."

Robert replied, "That is good, old friend. I am glad to know that your people are not involved. Unfortunately, the British are busy stirring up the native people in this area to make war against the settlers."

Wappanakuk's eyebrow lifted. "Indeed? Tell me more."

Robert explained, "We have learned that they sent representatives to the Creek Nation back in July to recruit them as allies against the Patriots. They paid them in silver and provided muskets and powder. We understand that some of their officers and soldiers have remained among them to take part in their attacks on frontier settlements."

"Is that why I encountered so very many people headed to the north and east? I came down through South Carolina and crossed the Savannah River at Augusta. I saw people in wagons and on foot moving inland and toward the coast."

"Yes. People have abandoned their homes and farms in great numbers. There have been numerous attacks and killings. Most were late last summer. Many crops, cabins, and barns have been burned."

Wappanakuk shook his head. "How tragic and senseless." He looked at their cabin and noticed the firing ports and the dirt piled against the logs. "I see that you have chosen to remain here and strengthen your home."

Robert nodded. "Yes, we have a fortress now. It is barely suitable for living, though. Mostly it is a fort for fighting. We still sleep in it, of course. Would you like to see what we have done?"

"Yes, indeed!"

The men all rose from the table and headed for the cabin. Wappanakuk whistled in awe when he saw the trenches and pit that they had dug inside.

"Gentlemen, this is most impressive, indeed. You have a very defensible fort. You have done well, my friends. But it is a shame that you have been forced to destroy the interior of such a lovely cabin."

"That's what I said!" chirped Milly.

"Still, Miss Milly, it is better to save your home than abandon it. Those trenches can be filled someday. Or better yet, you may keep them for a cellar or storage and build a wood floor right over the top of them," Wappanakuk encouraged.

"That is my plan," affirmed Robert. "But, come. That is enough talk about defenses and floors. Let us sit and visit. Supper will be ready soon. Let's head back to the table and see what the ladies have prepared for the evening meal."

The ladies did not disappoint. They served a sumptuous meal of fire-roasted chicken, potatoes fried in middling grease, fried corn cakes, and buttery squash. For drinks there was cold water, hot tea, and fiery rum for the men. The meadow full of family and friends ate heartily and conversed until darkness began to creep over the countryside. The temperature began to drop considerably.

They quickly cleaned the tables and dinnerware and retired to the cabin. Wappanakuk pitched his bedroll in the connecting trench between the cabin door and the central pit where the women and children slept. An hour later all of the candles were snuffed out and the cabin grew silent as everyone descended into deep, restful sleep.

CHAPTER NINE
THE RAID

Robert felt something pressing on his lips and nose. He opened his eyes and to his horror the red face of an Indian stared down at him. He began to kick and swing his arms, but he could not move ... he could not scream.

"Robert, stop! It is I. It is Wappanakuk."

He stopped swinging his arms and stared wide-eyed at his friend.

Wappanakuk raised his finger to his lips, urging Robert to remain quiet.

He hissed softly, "Robert, there are men in the woods outside the cabin. I believe that an attack is coming."

"How do you know there are men in the woods?" asked Robert.

"I smelled them. And I heard them."

Just as Wappanakuk spoke a horse emitted a nervous whinny from the direction of the barn. Robert's eyes grew wide.

"How many do you think are out there?"

"I do not know, but it must be several. Their smell is strong. They are men of the forest, no doubt the Creek Indians that you have long feared. It sounded like they were laboring and dragging something very heavy through the woods."

"Dragging something heavy? What could that be?" asked Robert.

"Most likely a battering ram. They will try to break down your door with a heavy timber. We must wake the others quietly. No talking. No candles. We do not want to alert them to the fact that we are aware of their presence."

Robert joined Wappanakuk in the task of waking everyone. They crawled quietly through the trenches, silently waking each defender and informing them of the situation. After rousing the men in the outer trench, Robert crawled quietly into the pit to wake up the younger boys and warn Milly and Esther. Little Robert took his position at the northern firing port. Joshua, and John sleepily reported to east and south sides of the cabin to serve as musket and rifle loaders.

It took less than five minutes for all of the men and boys to reach their assigned positions. The lookouts peered through the firing holes, looking for any sign of movement. There was no moon. It was pitch black outside, except for the soft glow of the stars that illuminated the clear sky.

Robert conferred with Wappanakuk. He was unsure how to deal with the Indian threat. "What should we do now?"

"You do nothing until you can see them. They may only be scouting out your farm, or perhaps they are planning to steal your horses and livestock. You will know their intentions if and when they open fire on your cabin."

"So we just wait?" asked Robert, exasperation adding to his nervousness.

"No. We do not have to wait. There is something else that we can do. You must let me sneak out of the cabin and move around behind them. I will scout their positions. If their intent is hostile, I can fight better in the forests and fields than I can from behind these walls. I may be able to distract them and make them think that they are outflanked or perhaps even outnumbered."

"Oh, no, my friend. I cannot ask you to do that. I cannot ask you to fight our battle for us, especially if you are unprotected and out in the open."

"You have not asked, Robert. If this battle is yours, then this battle is mine. You are my companions and friends. And, besides, I owe your son a blood debt that can never be repaid."

"Are you sure that you can get outside undetected?"

"Yes, of course. But we must make haste. If we wait until an actual attack begins, then it will be too late."

Robert nodded grudgingly. "All right then, Wappanakuk. All I can say is that I am very grateful for your help." The men shook hands. "Which direction will you go?"

"I will move toward the northeast corner at the front of the cabin. The sounds that I heard came from the southwest side, more in the direction of your barn. Perhaps they will try to take your livestock and leave the cabin alone."

Robert nodded hopefully. "That would be good. Cows and horses can be replaced."

Wappanakuk cautioned, "But I must first tell Lewis what my plans are, since he is standing watch on the northeast side. I must cross in front of his firing hole in order to reach the trees. I do not want him to shoot me. And you must inform the others that I will be outside the cabin."

"Very well then," Robert replied. "I will meet you at the door."

It took a couple of minutes to pass the word that Wappanakuk was sneaking out of the cabin. Robert and Frank moved to the trench directly below the door. They quietly removed the two protective timbers from their brackets and placed them across the trench. Robert gripped the leather latch string and prepared to let their friend out into the darkness.

As the Indian knelt in the trench beside Robert he checked his equipment. He had his two flintlock pistols tucked into his belt. In his right hand he held his razor-sharp hunting knife. In his left hand was his tomahawk. A smaller dagger dangled in its sheath, suspended by a leather cord around his neck. He crawled onto the edge of the door platform and prepared to exit the cabin.

"I am ready, Robert. Pull the latch and open the door. But only a few inches. We do not want them to see any movement of the door."

Robert applied slight downward pressure to the leather string and silently lifted the heavy latch from its cradle. He had barely opened the door when Wappanakuk slithered silently through the gap. He was amazed at how easily the stealthy Waccon warrior squeezed through a crack barely over six inches wide. Wappanakuk crawled to his left and disappeared into the night. Robert shut the door quickly, and then he and Frank placed the timber security bars back into their brackets.

Lewis's heart was in the bottom of his throat. He could hear the blood whooshing through his ears as he peered through his firing port, looking for any sign of life or movement in the trees. He was also waiting for Wappanakuk to cross in front of his position.

He had actually calmed down a bit from the excitement of his father waking him and telling him that hostiles were outside the cabin. For those first few minutes his hands had shaken uncontrollably.

So now Lewis waited. He scanned the tree line, looking for any sign of life or movement. There was nothing. Moments later Wappanakuk's buckskin clothing filled Lewis's field of sight through his firing hole. Even though Lewis knew that he was coming and fully expected him, the sudden appearance of movement right in front of his face startled him. Then, just as quickly as he appeared, Wappanakuk disappeared from view.

"He must be in the woods by now," thought Lewis. The boy uttered a silent prayer for his Indian friend.

Robert was manning the firing hole to the right of the cabin door. He had a solid view directly to the east and could see a little bit to the south. He was beginning to wish that he had installed more firing ports with better fields of view.

Suddenly the woods to his right erupted in sparks and light. Someone was striking a flint! Then small, bright yellow flames caught fire somewhere beyond the edge of the tree line.

He shouted, "I see fire to the southeast! They're going to try to burn us out!"

The Indians released flaming arrows into the air. There were several dull thuds on the roof.

"I see them!" responded Frank, who was manning the lone firing hole on the southern side of the cabin.

The eerie battle screams of the Creeks commenced. It sounded like the woods to the south and southeast were full of them.

Suddenly screaming and crying of women and babies erupted within the central pit of the cabin. Esther wailed uncontrollably. The baby girls followed her lead.

"Goodness, Esther! Shut your mouth!" screamed Milly. "Robert, how many of the savages are there?"

Robert didn't have time to answer. He swiftly aimed his .54 caliber Virginia rifle at the direction of the origin of the flames and fired. He heard a scream of pain and knew that his shot had found its mark. Less than a second later Frank fired his musket in the same direction.

Frank passed his expended musket to John. "Johnny, load it with buckshot. I want to scatter as much lead into the trees as I can." John traded his Brown Bess musket for Frank's second weapon, an old .69 caliber French Charleville musket. Frank aimed through the firing hole again and squeezed the trigger as John quickly reloaded the Brown Bess.

Then the Creeks opened fire. The heavy lead balls thudded against the logs above Robert and Frank's firing holes. They sounded like fingers thumping on ripe watermelons. Other projectiles sailed harmlessly into the protective dirt mounds beside their holes. Some stray earth flew through the openings, but the firing of the Indians was ineffective.

"I can't see anything at all!" yelled Chris, sounding frustrated. He was running back and forth between the two firing holes on the west side, looking for a target.

"I think they're all on this southeast corner! But keep a good lookout, they might shift around." yelled Robert. "Robbie, do you see anything?"

"No, Papa!" Little Robert was watching through his hole on the north side.

"Milly, get up in the trench with Junior! If he begins to shoot, you can reload for him. If Lewis begins to shoot, move over and reload for him. Just do the best you can. Leave the babies with Esther!"

"Yes, Robert!" she yelled in response.

"Chris, if they move around to your side, we will shift holes and adjust our fire. Just keep watching. If we need you over here I will let you know."

"All right, Robert!" Chris responded from the opposite trench.

Robert and Frank continued to pour their shots into the trees as John and Joshua reloaded for them. They didn't know if they were hitting anything or not, but they kept up the firing. The two sides exchanged shots for about ten minutes.

Then, as quickly as the commotion began, it seemed to stop. Everything became quiet. It felt like an eternity of silence. Ten minutes later the combat resumed. The woods thundered with gunfire.

Suddenly Lewis shouted, "Papa! They're coming toward the front of the cabin!"

Lewis spotted the Indians as they burst from the trees. There were three of them. They ran silently. Lewis took aim at the Indian closest to him and fired his .36 caliber rifle. He heard the impact of the ball as it struck the Indian in the center of his chest. The man screamed in pain, but kept running. Lewis stared through the hole, watching the Indian run through the smoke of his rifle. He was mesmerized ... almost frozen ... as the man ran straight at him. Then his father shot the Indian on the far right.

The Indian that Lewis wounded screamed as he continued his run toward Lewis's hole. That scream snatched Lewis out of his mental freeze. He jerked his rifle back inside the hole and was reaching for his second weapon, an old .75 caliber trade musket, when a barrel came thrusting into the hole right beside his face. Lewis reacted immediately, instinctively grabbing the barrel of the gun with his left hand and trying to wrestle it from his enemy. He pulled inward and downward, deeper into the trench beside him. He simultaneously forced the barrel away from his face.

On the other side of the log wall the wounded Indian pulled the trigger. The rifle belched a massive cloud of smoke and fire into Lewis's face. He screamed in pain yet held on to the barrel as it heated blazing hot in the palm of his hand. The explosion blew his hat off of his head and scorched his eyebrows and face. The ball only traveled twelve inches and impacted harmlessly into the rear wall of the trench.

The invisible enemy beyond the wall tugged at his rifle, attempting to pull it back out, presumably to reload. But Lewis held a firm grip and downward pull on the barrel. Amazingly, a bronze colored hand appeared through the opening. In that hand was a cocked pistol.

Lewis reached out with his other hand and grabbed the barrel of the pistol, but the Indian was strong. As he held fast to the barrels of both weapons, he opened his mouth and propelled his head forward onto the Indian's exposed hand. He bit down hard just behind the thumb. Lewis tasted the man's salty blood. He growled with determination and then in desperation he bit down even harder. He heard a bone crack somewhere in the attacker's hand.

The Indian screamed and released his grip on the pistol. Lewis caught the weapon, flipped it around in the air, and pulled the trigger as he stuck it into his firing hole.

The outward pressure against the rifle released. The Indian had stopped pulling. Lewis jerked the gun through the hole and tossed it on the floor of the cabin behind his trench. He looked through the hole but couldn't see anything but complete darkness.

Robert heard the sounds of fighting coming from his left. He heard Lewis yelling, grunting, and growling. He heard a shot and a shrill scream and then saw the flash of a shot inside the cabin.

He shouted, "Lewis, are you all right? Are you injured?"

"I'm fine, Papa. My hand is scorched and I have some powder burns on my face, but I'm all right."

"Thank God!" his father responded.

"I can't see anything outside!" Robert yelled, exasperated. "What about you, Lewis?"

"I can't see anything, either! There's a dead Indian in front of my hole!"

Lewis had just responded to his father when the doorframe and crossbars of the front door cracked. An invisible force, massive in size and power, had impacted the cabin door from the outside.

"The savages are going to break through the door!" screamed Milly.

"Don't worry, dear, they will never break through those oak beams. And the door is simply too thick and strong," Robert assured her.

But he was wrong ... horribly and dangerously wrong. Seconds later another mighty impact slammed against the wood. The center of the door bowed inward as the lower crossbeam cracked in the middle.

"The beam is broken!" shouted Chris. "One more hit like that one and they'll break through!" He grabbed his rifle and musket and jumped out of his trench. He made his way into the pit with Esther and the children. He flipped the bed up on its side and screamed, "Esther! Get the babies behind the bed! Stay out of sight from the door! And for goodness sake, keep them quiet!"

He knelt down at the mouth of the connecting trench, where he had a full view of the door and leaned his musket against the wall of the pit to his right. He cocked his rifle, aimed at the door, and waited.

Seconds later the battering ram struck the door again. The bottom beam exploded inward as the center of the door gave way. The thick wood panels cracked down the center along a seam.

Creek warriors poured through the ruptured door. The women and children screamed in horror. Explosions erupted throughout the cabin as Chris, Robert, and Frank fired at the intruders.

Robert screamed a warning to his son, "Lewis, hide in the trench! Go quickly! Indians have gotten into the house!"

Lewis heard his father's shout and darted around the corner into the side trench. He tried as best he could to melt into the wall of the trench and hide. He was so afraid. He was completely alone. And he wasn't sure how many of his family and friends remained alive inside the cabin. He pointed his rifle toward the corner of the trench and waited.

Lewis jumped in fear when an Indian came running around the corner. The man saw Lewis and reacted immediately. He threw up his pistol and fired. Lewis felt the warmth of the muzzle blast in his face and a searing fire in his left arm. Still, Lewis pulled the trigger on his rifle. The Indian gave a mighty lurch and then stumbled forward, slamming head-first into Lewis. The boy flipped backward under the weight of the Indian. His attacker had been hit, but he was not dead. The man screamed in a strange language and grasped at Lewis's neck.

Lewis felt the powerful grip of the Indian's hands around his neck. His skin stretched with pain. He gasped for a breath but could not find one. He began to see tiny twinkling lights that almost looked like stars against the darkness of the cabin ceiling. His brain was becoming devoid of oxygen and he was on the edge of unconsciousness.

"He is going to strangle me!" Lewis thought with horror.

His survival instincts kicked in. He tightened the muscles in his neck to resist the crushing grip of the Indian. He searched for every ounce of strength left in him and focused that strength on his right leg, which he kicked at his attacker. The Indian grunted in pain and rolled slightly to his right.

That was all of the opening that Lewis needed. He reached down with his right hand and whipped his knife out of his belt. He quickly jabbed the knife into the Indian's back.

Then he blacked out.

Lewis heard voices. He felt water splashing in his face. His somehow managed to open his tired eyes. He saw Wappanakuk hovering over him and was confused at first. Lewis smiled when he saw his mother and father and little brother, Robert, all gathered close around him.

He tried to speak but his neck was sore and swollen. The inflamed tissues around his vocal cords muffled his words. He grumbled as best he could, "Is it over? Did we get them all?"

Wappanakuk placed a firm hand on his chest, "Yes, Tarowa Yetashta, our enemies are slain. You and your family are safe. You fought most bravely, Little Warrior."

Robert and Milly scooped up their boy from the ground and wept as they held him close.

CHAPTER TEN
A BEAUTIFUL INDIAN GIRL

Not everyone survived the horrible attack by the Creek Indians. Both Chris and Esther Chandler died in the attack, leaving an orphaned son. Robert and Milly would have another little boy to raise in the Hammock home.

Wappanakuk and Lewis left before sunrise the next morning to go to Wrightsborough and fetch back the local militia to the scene of the battle. Robert believed that the size of the attack was serious enough to justify involving the army. He also discovered that the muskets and pistols carried by the Creeks were stamped with a large, "GR," the stamp of the army of Great Britain.

The Creeks had attacked the Hammock home with weapons supplied by the Redcoats!

Several hours later they heard the sounds of horses and wagons on the road. Soon Wappanakuk and Lewis rode into the clearing, followed by three wagons containing about a dozen men, none of them armed. Four other men followed on horseback. Those four were well armed.

"We have brought help, Robert," Wappanakuk declared. "The Quakers have come to help bury the dead. And there are four men from the militia company of Captain Robert Carr. They insisted upon coming along to see if they might be of help."

"Good," Robert responded. He looked with concern at Lewis. "Are you all right, son? I've been worried about you."

"I'm fine, Papa. Just a little sore." His voice sounded scratchy and hoarse. "Wappanakuk checked my arm and put on a poultice and fresh dressing while we were in town. He said it's looking just fine."

Robert smiled at his son and then turned his attention to the visitors from town. One of the men was Joseph Maddock, leader of the Quaker settlement in Wrightsborough. He had brought several men from his church with him to help bury the Indians.

A burly militiaman climbed down from his horse and extended a handshake to Robert.

"Mr. Hammock, I'm Sergeant Zachariah Henderson of Captain Carr's company of militia. We've been trying to get around to all the homesteads that haven't been abandoned and check on people. We were in town when your boy and his Indian friend came riding in. We decided that we would ride on out with the burying party and see how we might be of help."

"I wish you had been here last night, Sergeant. We could have used the help then, for sure."

The sergeant looked at the row of covered bodies in the yard. "Looks to me like you folks did a fair job on your own." He grinned broadly, exposing crooked, discolored teeth.

"It was not without great loss. We must bury our dearest friends today."

"I'm mighty sorry for those folks. Let's get these

Indians in the ground and then we can bury your friends nice and proper."

"I think you should first look at the weapons that they carried, Sergeant. They are all stamped with the symbols of the British Crown," declared Robert.

The sergeant squatted over the pile of weapons and examined each one.

"Yep! These are British army issue guns." The man spat on the ground. "We been seeing them all up and down this frontier. Redcoats are supplying these guns. There can be no other explanation. The British are arming the Indians. When we fight these Indians here in Georgia, we are fighting in the American Revolution! That's how I see it, anyway."

Robert nodded. "I quite agree, Sergeant. King George is no friend of ours. England holds all of us colonials in a very low regard. The simple truth is that we are not Englishmen, but Americans. I believe that the only option that we have left is to fight."

"I agree," said the Sergeant. "But Mr. Hammock, folks like you can't go it alone out here on the edge of Creek lands. You don't have enough neighbors to stand together and fight. You were lucky last night, but I don't believe your luck will hold out for you a second time."

"What are you saying, Sergeant?"

"I'm saying that it's time for you to pack up your wife and children and bring them into Captain Carr's Fort. We have a fine fort built at the captain's place. There's room enough for close to three hundred settlers. You need to get inside those walls with us to make your stand."

"I'm not quite ready to leave my home just yet, Sergeant."

"I'm just making an offer, Mr. Hammock. And the offer will stand until you're ready to take us up on it. We'll open up the gates for you when you come. Just head north up Reedy Creek and cross the Little River, then turn northwest. It's about seven or eight miles from here."

"I'm grateful, Sergeant. We just might take you up on that offer. Not right now, but someday."

The men soon began the gruesome task of burying the Indians who had died in the battle. Even with the help of the men of the militia and the Quakers the job took several hours. It was early afternoon when the Quakers returned to Wrightsborough. Robert invited the militiamen to join him back at his cabin.

As they rode into the yard they saw Milly and the children standing near the cabin. She walked over and greeted the group.

"You men haven't had a bite to eat since breakfast, and it will be time for supper before we know it. I've set out a couple of loaves of bread and butter to hold you over. There's also fresh milk and hot tea."

"We don't need to take too long," Robert cautioned. "We need to bury our friends."

Milly nodded. "I fetched Esther's quilt to wrap them in. She told me some time ago that her mother made it for her. I know that it was dear to her. I only wish that we had proper caskets for them."

"That was very thoughtful of you, Milly. And very appropriate." He turned to the men. "Gentlemen, let us enjoy some food and then we will hold service for the Chandlers."

A half-hour later the men carefully and reverently placed Chris and Esther's bodies in the back of Robert's wagon. The Hammock family and guests then formed a short funeral procession and marched silently to a nearby grave plot. Robert led the group in a reverent service in honor of their dear friends.

An hour later the men were finished with the grave and made their way back to the Hammock cabin. Frank and

Lewis had a roaring campfire going in addition to Milly's cooking fire. Wappanakuk was "helping" Milly with the cooking, but from the exasperated look on her face he wasn't being very helpful, at all. The boys beckoned Robert and the soldiers to join them beside the fire. Within minutes the men were smoking pipes, telling stories, and laughing. Moments later Wappanakuk joined them. They were all in a strangely joyous mood after such a physically difficult and death-filled day.

Suddenly a scream pierced the air. It echoed through the forest to the west.

"What was that?" the sergeant exclaimed.

Milly came running around the corner of the cabin. "Robert, I heard a scream. Is it the Indians again?"

"That sounded like a woman!" one of the other militiamen replied.

"Might have been a wolf," volunteered one of the other soldiers.

Wappanakuk shook his head. "No. That was most definitely human. It sounded like a woman to me, as well. Somewhere to the west."

"We have to go and see what it was," Robert declared.

Another scream, somewhat weaker than the first, came from deep in the woods. Everyone's eyes grew wide.

"I'm not going out in those woods," one of the soldiers replied.

"Me either," echoed another.

Wappanakuk stood. "Robert, Frank, Lewis … come with me. We will search. Bring your weapons. You soldiers stay here and guard the cabin."

The four men grabbed their rifles and trotted off to the woods to the west.

"Let's spread out some," Robert suggested. "About fifty yards between us. Keep sight of one another."

Wappanakuk moved to the far left and Frank and Lewis moved to the far right. They all walked carefully, rifles at the ready. They strained to listen.

Lewis's heart was beating fast. He felt the rush of danger, much like he experienced the night before. He gripped his rifle tightly and continued through the underbrush. After he had traveled about a hundred yards he heard something off to his right. It sounded like a moan.

"Over here, Frank!" he hissed. He veered in that direction and then slowed down.

They came to the edge of a large depression in the forest floor. Frank and Lewis were not prepared for the sight that greeted their eyes in the bottom of that depression. There, with arms and legs wrapped around and tied to a small tree, was a young Indian girl.

The girl's eyes met Frank's and widened in fear. It looked like she was about to scream, but her eyes suddenly rolled backward into her head and she collapsed to her right. Her body dangled haphazardly beside the tree.

Lewis cupped his hands and yelled back to his left, "Papa! Wappanakuk! You'd better get over here!"

Frank carried the unconscious girl back to the cabin. Lewis carried both of their guns. Milly's eyes grew wide when she saw the beautiful young woman. She quickly placed a blanket near the fire and Frank laid her on it.

Milly looked up at the men surrounding the girl. "Now somebody tell me something! Where did she come from? Is she injured? Who is she and where did you find her?"

"Lewis and I found her in the bottom of a gully in the woods. She was wrapped around a tree and tied up tight. No telling how long she'd been there," explained Frank. He reached out with concern and felt for a pulse in her wrist, then brushed back the coal-black hair from her eyes.

"She is a Cherokee maiden," explained Wappanakuk. "I do not think she is injured. She is no more than thirteen or fourteen years old. She was most likely taken captive by the Creeks in the last few days. They simply tied her to the tree and, no doubt, planned to retrieve her after the attack on your farm."

"How do you know she is Cherokee?" asked Robert.

"By her clothing and beadwork. She is obviously Cherokee."

"Why would they take her? I thought the Cherokee and Creek were allies and tolerated one another," Robert observed.

"For the most part they are. I can only guess, but based upon her age she was probably just an easy opportunity for the war party."

"She certainly is a pretty girl," Frank stated. He was captivated by her beauty and had not taken his eyes off of her since he placed her on the blanket.

Wappanakuk grunted. "Yes, Frank, she is an beautiful young woman, and would be highly prized among the Creeks. One of them, no doubt, claimed her as a war prize and planned to make her his wife."

Milly soaked a small towel with the water and wiped it across the girl's face and neck. The Indian girl gasped at the cold and sucked in a deep breath. Her eyes fluttered open and she stared at Frank's dark face. Fear seized her and she began to kick and thrash beneath the blanket. Then the screaming began. The girl wailed with a broken, fearful, mournful cry.

Wappanakuk knelt beside her head and attempted to soothe her. He patted her arm and quietly hissed, "Tss, tss, tss …."

The girl calmed down somewhat and ceased her screaming, but retained her expression of horror. Then Wappanakuk began to speak to her in a tongue unfamiliar to Robert and the others. Relief washed across the girl's face and she conversed with Wappanakuk, asking questions in rapid-fire succession. Wappanakuk answered her questions patiently and kindly, and it was clear that he was asking questions, as well. The girl seemed to answer with candor. Everyone else stood by helplessly, observing the prolonged conversation.

After a few minutes the girl smiled and nodded in response to one of Wappanakuk's questions. He reached down and took her by the hand, helping her to sit upright. He and Frank gently draped the blanket around her shoulders. She instinctively scooted a bit closer to the warm fire.

Frank dipped a pewter mug into the bucket of water and handed it to her. She smiled and drained it quickly, then offered it back to Frank. She obviously wanted more. Frank filled her cup again and again she drank it dry. Finally satisfied, she pulled her knees up to her chest and wrapped her arms around them and then stared uncomfortably into the fire.

"Well ... tell us what else you two talked about," Robert demanded. "You carried on quite a conversation. We would like to know what was said."

"My guess was quite correct. The girl told me that the Creek warriors stumbled upon her in the woods near her home. The warriors took her three days ago. At least four of the men were unmarried. They spent the past three days arguing and bickering over who would have her as a wife. The matter was not yet settled. They tied her up in that deep gully early last night to prevent her escape while they made war upon your home."

"So she's been there for almost an entire day?" Milly exclaimed.

Wappanakuk frowned. "Yes. She had resolved herself to the fact that she was going to die beside that tree. Since so many hours had passed she did not think that anyone was going to return for her."

"Well, no wonder she is so filthy. We must get her washed immediately and get her into some clean, warm clothes. Robert, you and Frank must help me heat water and draw her a bath. We will set up the tub inside the barn so that she can have some privacy and I will stand watch at the door while she washes herself."

"What is her name?" Frank asked pointedly.

His abrupt, out-of-context question elicited silence and dumbfounded looks among the group.

"I have not asked her," Wappanakuk confessed.

"Well, ask her then. She's not a wild animal. She has a name. We need to stop talking about her and actually talk to her."

Wappanakuk knelt again beside the Cherokee girl to ask her name. *Do de tsa do ah?*

She responded, "Nanye-Hi."

Wappanakuk nodded and smiled at her, then repeated her answer. "She is Nanye-Hi. Her name means, 'goes about.' She must have the spirit of a wanderer and explorer."

"Non-yay-hee," Frank repeated. "Such a beautiful name." He extended his open palm toward the girl and smiled broadly at her. With his other hand he patted his own chest. He told her, "I am Frank. That is my name. Frank."

She stared at him curiously.

He said his name again. "Frank."

At last she smiled ever so slightly and placed her hand on top of his. Then she repeated his name with her soft, high-pitched voice, "Frank. *O si tsi de na da tso hi.*"

Frank looked excitedly to Wappanakuk for a translation.

He smiled and said, "She said that it is good to meet you, Frank."

No one thought it possible, but Frank's smile grew even wider.

To everyone's amazement and delight, eight months later the young slave named Frank married the Cherokee maiden named Nanye-Hi.

CHAPTER ELEVEN
BATTLE AT CARR'S FORT

It was about a year later when the Hammocks finally had to flee for their lives. All of their neighbors were gone. The Creek Indians had stolen most of their livestock and burned their barn. They simply could not stay on their farm any longer. They had to go to Carr's Fort. They no longer had a choice. But first they had to make it across the rain-swollen Little River.

The wagon bottomed out in the slow-moving water. It began to seep through the cracks in the floor and soak the cargo inside. Frank snapped the leather reins and talked soothingly to the team pulling the wagon. Nanye-Hi sat on the wagon seat beside him, her eyes wide with fear at the rising water. She was holding their infant son, Simeon. The stout little four-month-old was sucking on his fist and paying absolutely no attention to the excitement all around him.

Milly popped her head out from beneath the canvas flap behind Frank and screamed, "Robert! Water's coming into the wagon!"

Her husband brought his horse alongside them. He had a small red-brown calf lying across the pommel of his saddle. The frightened animal bellowed loudly and repeatedly for its mother.

"Yes, dear, I know it is, but there's nothing that we can do about it now. This is the best ford across Little River for five miles in either direction. We're on the deepest spot right now and will start moving up in just a minute or two. There's no turning back now. We'll just have to get dried out when we get to the fort."

"This is going to be absolutely horrible!" she wailed.

Robert tried to reassure his wife. "It will be fine. We planned for this. The food and perishables are on top of boxes and crates. We'll just have to dry a few blankets and items of clothing. It will be all right."

Robert nodded to Frank. "Let's pick up the pace, Frank."

"Yes, sir."

Ten minutes later they were across the Little River and on dry land once again. Robert halted the tiny convoy to check their belongings. It was as he thought. Less than an inch of water had invaded the wagon bed and the damage was minimal. After a few minutes of rest the family moved on toward the northwest. They had eight miles of rough travel ahead, and Robert wanted to reach Carr's Fort before sundown.

The Hammock family did not have much left to show for their four years of living in Georgia. The Indians and bandits had stolen most of their livestock and food stores. What little cornmeal and flour they had left was piled on top of wooden crates in the wagon. There were also a couple of bags of turnips and some other late season vegetables. Crocks of preserved food, dried venison, blankets, animal pelts, and tobacco barrels filled every nook and cranny of the wagon. Farm implements and tools were tied to the outside of the rig.

They only had four horses left. Two pulled the wagon while Robert and Lewis were mounted on the other two. They managed to salvage about a dozen chickens that the last group of marauders had left behind. And, amazingly, they had discovered the cow and calf wandering loose in the woods near the barn. The animals had, no doubt, inadvertently wandered off and escaped from the bandits in the darkness after the last night raid. The mama cow was tied to the back of the wagon. Once on dry land the calf trotted along behind her faithfully.

They followed a narrow but well-worn trail that ran along the banks of the Beaverdam Creek. It was just wide enough for the wagon and they encountered little difficulty during their brief trek. It was about two hours before dark when they crossed a tiny fork in the creek and saw the smoke and palisades of Carr's Fort. There were a couple dozen men and women working in the fields around the fort. All of the men were well-armed. A few minutes later they eased up to the gate, which was closed. Two men were on sentry duty, watching from platforms on either side of the gate.

The man on the left, a rather dirty fellow in a greasy, filthy hunting frock and black floppy hat, greeted them. "Good evening. Who are you folks?"

Robert spoke for the family. "I'm Robert Hammock. My place is about eight miles south of here along Reedy Creek. Why are the gates closed during daylight?"

"Well, we have had quite a bit of Indian trouble. One can't be too careful these days. What brings you to Captain Carr's Fort?"

"We got hit again at our place last night. Bandits cleaned out the last of our livestock. We just can't hold out on our own anymore. We figured that we would join up with the refugees here at the fort. We have a standing invitation from Sergeant Zachariah Henderson to come and join up at Carr's Fort whenever it became necessary. He told me that if we ever came you would open the gates for us."

"That so, huh? Let me check, then. Hold on just a bit." He turned and yelled toward the ground inside the fort, "Micah! Go get Zach Henderson! Tell him I need him on the gate right now!"

A few minutes later the familiar face of the rough and grizzly sergeant appeared beside the unwelcoming sentry.

"Amos, can't you even stand guard without needing something? Why did you call me up here on this wall? I was just about to eat my supper."

The fellow named Amos pointed down at the Hammock wagon. "This fellow says you gave him an invitation to come and move in here at the fort."

The sergeant squinted and examined the travelers. He didn't seem to recognize them at first.

"Sergeant Henderson, I'm Robert Hammock ... from Reedy Creek. You helped us bury that bunch of Creek Indians a while back."

A look of recognition washed across his face. He smiled broadly. "Mr. Hammock! Of course! So, you finally gave up trying to make it on your own?"

"We got cleaned out of most of our stores and livestock last night and decided to fold it in. We were hoping to ride out the war here with you folks."

"Yes, sir! And you are most welcome. Is that smooth-talking Indian still with you ... the one from Carolina?"

"No, Sergeant. He left us and went back home a few months ago."

"That's too bad. That Indian was one impressive fighter. He would have been a good scout to have here at the fort." He barked over his left shoulder, "Open up the gate!"

Moments later the pointed palisades at the top of the gate angled inward as the bottom angled out toward the Hammock wagon. There was much heaving and grunting as the gate swung up and locked in place overhead. Frank clucked at the team of horses and the wagon gave a lurch as it moved forward.

Robert sighed quietly and his heart ached with a dark sadness as they drove through the portal into the dim, wet fort. He was experiencing an overwhelming sense of failure and frustration. The Hammock family had a new home. He just hoped that it was a temporary one.

It was late afternoon on December 31, 1778. Robert and Frank were pulling their regular rotation on guard duty. They drew an assignment that neither of them cared much for ... gate watch. It was much easier to be manning one of the blockhouses or perches along the top of the wall. Gate duty required constant attention. Gate guards had to identify people, decide who should be allowed into the fort, and supervise the opening and closing of the gate. But at least they were eating well. Both of them had wooden plates piled high with smoked pork and fresh bread and mugs full of steaming hot tea. And it would be dark soon. Once the sun was down no one would be going into or out of the fort.

About an hour into their watch they heard a single rider break through the tree line to the east. The man was moving at a fairly high rate of speed, galloping across the fallow fields near the fort.

Robert called out, "Rider coming! Looks like militia! Open the gate!"

Below him a half-dozen men threw their shoulders into the heavy load of the gate and swung it upward. The rider's horse never broke stride. The man leaned sideways to lower his profile and rode full-speed through the partially opened gate. The men released the gate and allowed it to fall closed behind him. He drew his horse to a rapid stop and nimbly swung down from the saddle.

Sergeant Davis greeted the man. "I'm Mike Davis, sergeant of the guard tonight. And who might you be?"

"Ensign Andrew Willard, Wilkes County Militia. I bear a message for Captain Carr."

"I'm right here." Captain Robert Carr stepped out of his farmhouse, a large cabin that sat in the center of the fort palisades. He pulled on his heavy wool overcoat and wiped food from his mouth as he approached the messenger.

Ensign Willard snapped a salute. "Captain Carr, I have an urgent message from Colonel John Dooly in Augusta. He has dispatched messengers to all of the forts in the region."

"Verbal or written?"

"Written, sir."

He reached into his pouch and retrieved a letter. He placed it in the greasy hand of Captain Carr. The captain removed the binding string and broke the red wax seal. He read the message quickly, his eyes growing wide. He reached up with his right hand and covered his mouth, then exhaled and folded the letter closed. The crowd of men gathered around began to murmur.

Finally, one of the sergeants asked, "What is it Captain? What does it say?"

The captain looked grim. "Boys, we are no longer just dealing with Indians anymore. The Redcoat Colonel Archibald Campbell has landed a British force of over 2,000 soldiers on Tybee Island. They captured Savannah the day before yesterday. Campbell flanked Howe's force of six hundred men and took the city without artillery. Four hundred were captured. The capital was seized intact." He spat on the ground. "Get your affairs in order, boys. The Redcoats are occupying Georgia. They're in Savannah and will be after Augusta next."

"What do we do, Captain?" asked one of the men.

"Prepare yourselves for travel, gentlemen. We leave for Augusta at first light!"

Captain Carr's company of militia had been gone for less than a week when green-uniformed Tory militia swarmed into Carr's Fort. The British-led soldiers from Augusta rode in without any resistance. There were no able-bodied men to defend the fort. Carr had left a handful of toothless old men in charge. But it was clear that someone was chasing them. The Tories were under attack from outside the fort.

Lewis stood in the open doorway with his arms crossed, shaking his head. He couldn't believe what had just transpired before his very eyes. The old men of the fort had just handed over the garrison to the Tories without firing a single shot! Now Loyalist militiamen were swarming all over the walls and manning the firing ports, shooting excitedly in every direction at an unseen enemy in the fields beyond.

"At least someone has the guts to fight!" shouted Lewis.

Milly shouted at her oldest son. "Lewis Hammock! Get inside this blockhouse this very instant!"

Lewis stomped the wet dirt beneath his boots. He exclaimed, "Cowards!"

A nearby Tory lieutenant took issue with Lewis's proclamation. He stormed angrily toward him. "Boy, you need to watch your mouth. I'll not have you calling the King's soldiers cowards. I'll have your neck stretched if you don't mind your ways!"

Lewis stood his ground. "Sir, I wasn't calling you or your men cowards."

The officer stared at Lewis, puzzled. "To whom, then, were you referring?"

"I was referring to those old cowards who threw open the gates so that you egg-sucking Tories could just walk right in here and take our fort."

The lieutenant slapped Lewis across the mouth, knocking him into the log wall. The left side of his head smacked the wood with a resounding thud. He dropped to his hands and knees, dazed and woozy.

Milly Hammock appeared in the doorway and gasped at the sight of her son on the ground and the pool of blood that was forming beneath his nose and lips. She glared at the Tory officer as she reached down to help her son to his feet.

"Oh, what a fine, brave soldier you are, young man. Is this what the King's soldiers are about, waging war against women and children? You should be ashamed of yourself, you low down, filthy coward!"

"You watch your tongue, too, woman. I've never struck a female, but I will take great pleasure in striking you! Now take that boy inside and stay in there before I have both of you thrown in jail!"

Milly tugged at Lewis's hunting frock and yanked him inside the doorway. She angrily pushed him down onto the dirt floor against the outer wall of the fort.

"Lewis, if you don't mind … try not to get killed before your father returns home. Now stay seated on that floor and keep your mouth shut!"

"Yes, Mother."

"There's enough trouble both inside and outside the walls of this fort without you stirring up more of it. Do you understand?"

"Yes, Mother."

Milly calmed down just a little bit.

Nanye-Hi was sitting along the wall, taking care of the Hammock children and trying to calm their fears. She soon had them all singing a Cherokee song that she had taught them several months before. The distraction really seemed to help. But even the singing and clapping could not drown out the sharp thuds of lead projectiles striking the wall behind them or the explosions of flintlocks being fired in the room over their heads.

Lewis thought angrily, "That's good. Light 'em up, boys!"

Milly knelt down beside her son and placed her hand

on his knee. "Lewis, what did you say to that man to make him so upset?"

Lewis looked up at her. "Nothing much. I just called him an egg-sucking Tory."

Milly fought the urge to smile. Lewis didn't bother to fight the urge. He grinned broadly, his bloody teeth showing behind his swollen lips.

Inside the walls of the fort things calmed down dramatically after the initial invasion by the Tories. The Patriots beyond the walls seemed to have taken a break from firing at the fort. The Hammock women and children remained hidden in the lower lever of the southwest corner blockhouse.

About a half-hour later, the shooting started again. When the battle resumed Lewis found a crack in the logs that gave him full view of the field to the west. He watched in awe as three dozen brave men sprinted into the open and made their way toward a barn in the center of the field.

"Mama! Nanye-Hi! Our men are attacking! There are men trying to take that big log barn over toward the creek. Come and see!"

His mother responded, "Lewis, I'm not getting down on the ground and crawling around to look at a bunch of men shooting one another."

But Nanye-Hi crawled over to the spot where Lewis was peeking through the wide crack in the logs.

"Look! There are some men who are down on the ground," commented Nanye-Hi. "And I hear the terrible cries of that one man. See how he is rolling around."

"He must be shot," Lewis acknowledged grimly. "But the other ones made it. Look! I see their smoke! The Patriots are starting to shoot!"

Sure enough, big puffs of blue and white rifle smoke began to belch from various openings in the barn. And soon men began firing from the roof, as well. Shouting and screams emanated from the interior of the fort. Several were screams of pain.

"Oh, they're putting it to them, now!" Lewis chattered excitedly. "I bet you they've got the angle down onto these bloody Tories."

"Lewis, watch your mouth! I will not have a son of mine talking like that!"

"Yes, Mother."

The firing inside the fort diminished as the shooting from outside the fort seemed to increase. They also heard a crescendo of shouting and shooting from the direction of the main gate, well outside of their personal field of view.

"Sounds like they're attacking from the front of the fort," Lewis observed. "With any luck we'll be free from these British lap dogs before sundown tonight."

Then Nanye-Hi shrieked, "Look! There's Frank!"

"What?" Lewis exclaimed. "How do you know it's Frank?"

"How many other African Georgia militiamen have you ever seen?" she retorted.

"Good point ..."

Suddenly Milly felt the urge to get down on the ground and join them. Joshua, John, and Robert were soon looking for cracks to peep through, as well. They all watched in awed silence as Frank sprinted across the open field. He ran directly to the screaming, wounded man who lay exposed to the enemy's fire.

They watched in amazement as Frank picked up the wounded man and ran toward the safety of the distant tree line.

Then they saw Frank fall. He was in an all-out run when his body lurched and tumbled. His forward momentum tossed the wounded man that he was carrying into the tall grass and weeds along the edge of the field. Frank lay motionless in the dirt.

Nanye-Hi screeched when she saw her husband go down. Lewis stared in disbelief. Milly was in shock.

"He's not moving! Why isn't he moving?" Lewis shouted.

Then they saw a very large white man leap out of the grass, grab Frank beneath his armpits, and pull him into the cover of the grass and trees beside the creek.

Nanye-Hi spun around and dropped against the log wall. She unleashed a loud, shrill Indian scream and then buried her face in her hands and wept.

CHAPTER TWELVE
BACK AT THE HOMESTEAD

"Where are they going?" asked Milly.

"It looks like they're leaving!" exclaimed Lewis.

Lewis and his mother watched the Tories through a large crack in the door. The uniformed men were lining up in formation. There were several wounded men sitting on horses or lying on makeshift litters. Drummers began to play crisp beats upon their drums.

"Why do you think they are leaving, Lewis?"

"I don't know, Mama. We haven't heard any shooting for a while. It sounds like our army might have left. Or maybe the Tories have just had enough and are going back to Augusta. I don't know."

They watched the men open the main gate and then march slowly out of the fort. Milly insisted that they wait until they could no longer hear the drums before they attempted to go outside the fort walls.

After several minutes Lewis proclaimed, "I'm tired of waiting!"

He threw open the door and headed for the gate. Nanye-Hi was right behind him. Soon dozens of women and children were pouring out of cabins and shacks and heading toward the opening. They walked outside and saw the remains of the battle that had raged beyond the walls. Wagons, debris, dead horses, and men littered the battlefield.

Moments later a tall, dark-skinned man stepped out of the woods to the east.

Lewis yelled, "Look!"

Nanye-Hi spun around and saw her husband across the field. She screamed, "Frank!" and took off running toward him. She sprinted across the field as fast as she could, weeping with joy every step of the way, and then she tumbled into his arms.

The Georgia militia was gone. They left their wounded behind and set off in pursuit of a Tory army out of South Carolina. Carr's Fort was quiet once again.

Frank was one of the wounded men who remained behind. He sat in a dilapidated rocking chair beside the fireplace in the blockhouse that was serving as the fort's hospital. There were two other wounded men in the room along with two very sick children. The little ones had some kind of fever and were being kept separate from the others in a far corner of the dark room. Their mothers attended to their care.

Nanye-Hi hovered over Frank, checking his blankets, adjusting the very thin pillow that cushioned his back, and keeping his mug full of hot tea with honey.

Frank protested, "Nanye-Hi ... my darling ... I'm fine. Please stop. Just sit down and talk to me. I don't need any more medical care."

His Cherokee bride sighed her frustration and then plopped down on the floor beside him, sitting cross-legged beside the warm fire. She gently leaned her head sideways and laid it on his knee. Frank stroked her dark black hair.

"When do you think Robert will return?" she asked.

"I don't know. No one has heard from them for three days. He might be somewhere up in South Carolina by now. There's no telling when he'll come back."

The heavy door of the blockhouse swung open and Lewis Hammock stepped inside, stomping the thick mud off of his feet.

"Lewis! Do not bring that mud inside the house! Go back outside right now and clean your filthy shoes!" scolded Nanye-Hi.

Lewis somberly turned around and stepped back outside for a moment. He quickly returned, but his black buckled shoes didn't appear to be any cleaner. Nanye-Hi rolled her eyes. Frank laughed.

"Where are you going, Lewis?" asked Frank.

"I'm just headed back to our shack after my shift on the wall. I thought that I would come by and see you and bring some news!"

"What news?" asked Frank. He sat up straighter, his attention piqued.

"Papa and the other men are back in the area. They didn't catch the Tories in South Carolina, but they've been chasing them for three solid days. They finally caught them! And they gave them a sound whipping in a battle at Kettle Creek!"

"They won the battle?" asked Frank.

"It was a total victory!" Lewis paused. "But still no word about Papa. I don't know if he is all right, or not. Mama's going to be worried sick. She's been a mess ever since he left."

"Mr. Robert is just fine. I'll pray for him," encouraged Frank. He stared into the dancing fire. "But how I do wish I had been there with him."

"Me, too," mused Lewis.

Robert Hammock was just fine, indeed. He survived the Battle of Kettle Creek without any injuries. He was actually something of a hero because he helped Colonel Elijah Clarke on the battlefield after the colonel's horse was shot from beneath him.

A few days later Robert and all of the other men of Carr's Fort were back behind the walls, safe and sound. Life gradually returned to normal ... which included patrols in the nearby woods and guard duty at the fort.

Robert and Frank were supposed to be on guard duty. It surprised Lewis somewhat when he woke up and heard his parents talking in the darkness. He soon heard why his father was not up on the fort wall. He had forgotten his pipe and had made a quick run back to the shack to get it.

Robert was just opening the door to leave and return to his guard post when a loud shot exploded outside. He threw open the door and looked to see what was happening. The alarm bells began to sound.

Robert cupped his hands and yelled, "What is it, Frank?"

"Indians!"

Frank was feverishly reloading his musket.

"How many?"

"At least a hundred! Maybe two! There's way too many! I don't think we can stop them!"

Frank angled his musket downward and fired another load of buck and ball at the enemy in the field beyond the wall.

Robert stuck his head back inside their shack. The children were awake. Lewis and Robbie were pulling on their breeches.

"Robert, what is it?" Milly wailed.

117

"Creeks. Maybe two hundred of them."

"Oh, my! They will swarm this fort!"

"We're not sticking around to find out. Milly, grab everything you can and get the children ready! Lewis, go hitch up our team to the wagon. I have it sitting beside the rear entrance. Get our horses and have them saddled, tied off, and ready to ride. Robert, you go get Nanye-Hi and Simeon. Boys, I want you to get everyone and everything loaded as fast as you can and be ready to go when Frank and I get there. Do you understand?"

Both boys responded, "Yes, Father."

Robert kissed his wife on the cheek. "It's going to be all right, my love. Just get everything together as fast as you can. I'll get us out of here."

Robert darted out the door and headed back to the wall. Dozens of men were firing into the wave of attackers. The wounded and dying among the defenders began to drop from the palisades and rooftops. Fire and death were raining down upon Carr's Fort.

Less than an hour later Carr's Fort was destroyed. It was burned to the ground by the attacking Creeks. Over a hundred souls perished in the attack, including their commander and host, Captain Robert Carr.

Fortunately, some families had the opportunity to escape in the darkness. The Hammock family, because of the quick work of Lewis and Robert, Jr., was one of the first groups to evacuate. They were well beyond the open field and on the northern road, riding deep under the cover of the trees, before the Creeks even knew that anyone had escaped the burning fort.

Lewis snapped the reins and guided the wagon back toward the Hammock home on Reedy Creek. With Carr's Fort destroyed, they had nowhere else to go.

Milly washed her hands in a large wooden bowl. She was preparing to begin work on the meals for the day. It was no small task to feed a household with so many hungry residents.

"Lewis, we need some fresh meat. I need you and Robbie to see what you can rustle up for the pot. There have to be some stray rabbits or a deer somewhere in these woods."

The boys jumped up from their pallets and began to layer on their clothes. They each donned a heavy linen hunting frock.

"Now don't go running out into the cold forest without some food in your belly. There's hot porridge over the fire."

"Yes, Mama," Lewis replied. He looked around the dark room. "Where's Papa?"

"He and Frank left out before daybreak to run over to Zachariah Phillips' fort. They're looking for news about the war, and to see if anyone has heard from Colonel Clarke. They should be back this afternoon, well before dark."

"Why didn't they wake me? I would have liked to have gone with them," complained Lewis.

"Your father knew that I needed you here. He couldn't leave us unprotected now, could he?"

Lewis's chest swelled just a bit. He liked the notion of being the man of the house, at least for a morning. And a man had to provide for his family. So Lewis needed to get to get busy with the task of hunting. He pulled on his shoes and then scurried over to the fireplace. He carefully removed the iron lid from the pot that hovered on a rack over a thin bed of coals. The fragrant steam of the porridge escaped into the cool air of the cabin. Lewis quickly ladled a bowl full of the dense mixture for himself and one for Robert, Jr.

"Eat up, Robbie. We need to get in the woods before the sun gets too high."

Both boys sat on either side of the fireplace and rested their backs against the log wall. Milly looked at her two growing sons and sighed. She longed for a proper home for her children and a proper table to take their meals. But for now they made do with their tiny lean-to cabin built onto the outside wall of Frank and Nanye-Hi's home.

It was mid-March, 1780. A year had passed since the destruction of Carr's Fort and the most recent displacement of the Hammock family. Their return home after their narrow escape from the fort had not been a joyous one. They found that their property had been pillaged. Their cabin and barn were burned almost to the ground. But in their despair they did find a small blessing. Frank's little cabin had not been bothered. It was, apparently, undiscovered by Tory and Creek raiders.

So they piled into the cramped space for several days while Robert and Frank worked to add a temporary expansion. They salvaged quite a few sections of logs from the burned structure of the Hammock cabin. They had to cut a few more trees to complete the work, as well as haul several loads of creek stone to construct a proper fireplace. But they managed to finish a livable, if not spacious, home for the Hammocks to occupy until circumstances changed. Of course, Frank and Nanye-Hi occupied their original side of the cabin, along with their toddler son, Simeon, and a very vocal six-month-old girl named Anna.

The two family units had combined their efforts of labor and spent the past year in survival mode. They hunted and fished, planted a small garden, and harvested a tiny crop of corn. Times were extremely tough, but they were getting by ... better than most people who still remained in the Georgia backcountry.

Their best defense was anonymity. As far as they could tell, no one knew that they were hiding so close to their old home site. The attacks upon homesteads and forts by the Tories and their Creek allies had been ongoing throughout the past year, but the Hammocks had somehow managed to avoid scrutiny. Milly thanked God every day for the relative peace that they had enjoyed for the past year.

Milly smiled at her sons. "Just leave your bowls by the fire, boys. I'll clean them for you. And be sure to take some of the corn cakes with you. You're sure to get hungry in an hour or two. I cooked them with some of the dried onions ... just like you like them, Lewis."

Lewis licked his lips. He and Robbie unwrapped the cloth bundle that sat atop the small stand beside the fireplace and each removed a handful of the flat, greasy cakes. They each wrapped them in a fresh piece of cloth and then stuffed them in their haversacks. Less than a minute later they grabbed their flintlocks and hats and shot out the door.

"Wait," Lewis whispered. "Let her get past that little tree."

Robert trembled with excitement. The boys were low on the ground, concealed behind a large fallen tree. A crooked spot in the trunk of the tree had created a small opening that gave them a view of the creek below. Lewis had hunted from this makeshift blind before, and he knew that it overlooked a well-worn deer trail that led to a perfect drinking spot along the creek. The numerous tracks confirmed that deer had been there recently. So it came as no surprise when this doe ambled down the trail an hour after they had settled in for the hunt.

"Steady, Robbie. Control your breathing. Remember, the tiniest wiggle can cause you to miss. Aim just above her front leg. Pick a tiny spot and aim at it."

Little Robert exhaled quietly as he tried to calm his nerves. He cradled the .36 caliber rifle in his left hand and sighted down the barrel. He squeezed the trigger ever-so-gently and the rifle barked. The boys were temporarily blinded by the cloud of white smoke that exploded from the pan and muzzle of the gun. They both jumped to their feet, attempting to see through the smoke and find if the shot had been true. Robert let go a shout of glee when he saw the wounded deer thrashing on the ground beside the water.

Milly smiled when she heard the shot. She knew that her boys would be bringing supper home. She hummed a jolly tune as she quietly busied herself with her work. The other children were still sleeping. She knew that it was getting a bit late in the morning for them to be lounging in the bed, but she reveled in the peace of their sleep and the solitude of her own thoughts.

But the peace and solitude that they had enjoyed for the past year was about to come to an end. The British and their Tory and Creek allies were about to descend upon the Georgia frontier with a mighty vengeance.

Part III

1780 - Over the Mountains

CHAPTER THIRTEEN
FREEDOM FOR FRANK

Robert rode his horse into the clearing near the cabin. The setting was peaceful. Frank and Lewis were tending to their slowly growing flock of cows, goats, and chickens. Milly and Nanye-Hi, with plenty of help from the children, were working in the garden.

The children screamed with delight when they saw their father riding down the trail and took off running toward him. He threw his leg over the horse's neck and slid down off of the animal. He knelt down to receive a barrage of hugs from his little ones. They had a lot of catching up to do. He had been away from home for five long days.

Milly followed slowly behind the children. As she walked toward Robert she wiped the sweat from her forehead with the back of her dirt-covered arm, leaving a gray streak in its place. Robert chuckled at the sight of her. She planted her fists firmly on her hips and tried to make a angry face, but she was so happy to see her husband that she couldn't maintain the frown. She patiently waited her turn for his attention. At long last he shuffled toward her with several little children dangling from his legs and grabbed her in a loving embrace.

"I've missed you," she whispered in his ear.

"I've missed you so much more," he countered.

Milly took Robert by the hand, leading him toward the table and benches in the yard. "Come, husband. Tell us what has happened. What are the British doing? How will it all affect us?"

Robert straddled the bench while everyone else gathered around the table, anxious to receive news from the outside world. Frank and Nanye-Hi sat down on the ground near Robert.

"Well, it seems that the only thing they are concerned with right now is controlling the residents of the backcountry and fortifying their military buildings and forts. The Tory Colonel Brown is working hard at building up the defenses of Augusta."

"Augusta? How do you know about Augusta? I thought you had to report to Wrightsborough," commented Lewis.

"I did go to Wrightsborough. That's where I had to swear my oath to King George."

There was an audible gasp from Milly and the older boys.

"You swore an oath to King George of England?" exclaimed Lewis. He was shocked. He could not believe that his father would do such a thing. He fought the urge to cry. Could it be possible? Was his father a traitor to the American cause?

His father placed a hand on his shoulder and nodded. "I had to, son. They gave me no choice. It was either that or prison … or maybe forced service in the Royal Navy. At least by swearing my oath I got to come home and keep my weapons."

"But an oath to King George!" complained Lewis. "I'll never forgive the Redcoats for the way they treated Frank.

How could you, Father? Don't you believe in an independent United States anymore?"

"Of course I do, son. More than ever. But the British are in total control of Georgia now. I did what I had to do in order to survive and stay home with my family. Surely you understand that."

Lewis nodded, but deep down in his heart he really did not understand. He was angry ... angry at the British, and now angry at his father.

"What about Congress?" asked Milly. "What about the Declaration of Independence?"

Robert shrugged. "I guess a piece of paper is only as strong as the army you have to back it up. The war is going bad for the Patriot cause. Washington is on his heels in the North. Cornwallis is running loose in the Carolinas and now he's sending at least eight hundred Redcoats to Georgia. It looks like we're beaten, at least for now. It will take a miracle to turn things around, I think."

"You mentioned Augusta," Frank reminded him. "Why did they make you go there?"

"They didn't make me go to Augusta. I went of my own accord."

"Why?" challenged Milly. "What possible reason did you have to go all the way to Augusta?"

"Well, there's an actual government there now. It's a British-controlled government, but it is functioning and attempting to serve the people. I went to the property office to file a document and get some papers."

"What papers? Is something else wrong that I need to know about?" Milly queried.

Robert smiled mischievously and shook his head. "No, my dear. Nothing is wrong. In fact, I think something has been made very right."

Milly stared at him. She was thoroughly confused.

Robert grinned broadly as he removed a set of crisply folded papers from the leather bag that hung on his side.

"Frank, these are for you."

Now Frank joined Milly in looking thoroughly confused. "For me? What are they?"

"These are papers of protection that declare you to be a free man. Freedom papers. I've named you and Simeon and Anna, since the law considered all three of you to be my property. You'll need to keep these with you at all times when traveling away from home."

Frank stared at him wide-eyed. "Mr. Robert, I don't understand."

Robert leaned toward him. "Frank, you're a free man now. You are no longer a slave, nor will you ever be again. I have released you from any and all legal attachments to me. No one will ever own you again."

Huge tears began to well up in Frank's eyes. The tears in his right eye overflowed and streaked down his shiny brown cheek. Nanye-Hi wrapped her arms around his neck and hugged him tightly.

"Well, say something, Frank!" Robert urged.

"I don't know what to say. You and Miss Milly have always been kind to me and made me feel like I was part of the family. You've never treated me like the other white folk seem to enjoy treating their slaves."

"Well, Frank, we've always considered you to be a part of this family. But now you have a family of your own. You're a man ... a good man. You have saved our lives and helped care for us for many years now. This was the least that I could do."

Frank hung his head low. He began to actually sob. "So what do I do now? Do I have to leave?"

"Frank, you can do whatever you want to," encouraged Milly. "You're completely free. Free to leave. Free to stay. Free to wait until you know what you want to do. Just free."

Lewis punched Frank in the shoulder. "I sure hope you don't leave. I don't know what I'll do without you."

Frank chuckled at Lewis and then looked into the eyes of his smiling wife. She kissed him on the end of his nose.

"What is your desire, husband?" asked Nanye-Hi. "What do you want to do?"

"I want to stay here with my family." He looked at Lewis and then at Robert. "After all, I am a Hammock, aren't I?"

Robert slapped both hands on his knees in approval and joy. "I was hoping you would say that. Because I have another set of papers for you." He reached into his bag. "This is the land claim of our dear friend Christopher Chandler, God rest his soul. The magistrate in Augusta assigned the lands to me because we have custody of his infant child. And I have, in turned, signed over his one hundred and fifty acres to you … if you want it."

Robert placed the papers in Frank's hand.

"It's my land?" Frank asked in disbelief.

"Yes, Frank. Your land. I have the deed right here. You just need to sign it. Of course, we neighbors will have to work together to make ends meet for quite some time, I suspect." Robert smiled broadly.

"I believe you're right," Frank responded.

"So what do you say, Frank? Shall we be neighbors?"

"No, sir. I like being family better."

Robert stood and reached his hand down to Frank and helped him to his feet. "Well, then, I guess all I can say is, 'Welcome home, Frank.'"

And they hugged. Former slave and master. Now neighbors. Now family.

Robert sat at the dinner table with Frank and Lewis and a rather distinguished-looking guest. Robert shook his head vigorously.

"I don't know, Colonel. Things have been mighty quiet this past month. And you're asking a lot. I had to swear my oath to King George and England a month ago.

If I take up arms again, it's a death sentence for me, pure and simple. They'll hang me. Cornwallis has declared it in writing. If I go to war against England again I will get the gallows with no mercy."

Colonel William Candler slapped the side of Robert's knee. "But, Robert, if we win this fight none of that will matter! Augusta is ripe for the picking. The Tory Colonel Brown has been slow in receiving support and men from Cornwallis. He has less than three hundred men to defend the town. We can run them out of upper Georgia once and for all, and maybe turn the tide of the war here in the South!"

"What about the Indians? I hear there are hundreds of Creek Indians flooding into Augusta for some big meeting with Brown. It doesn't matter how many troops Brown has if he has the Creek Nation on his side."

"They don't matter! They are a rabble, at best, and undisciplined. They'll run into the swamps and fields the moment they see our mighty army approaching," assured Colonel Candler.

Robert mulled the idea over. "And you say Colonel Clarke is in on this?"

"Yes, Robert. Most definitely. The assault is his plan and he will be in overall command. Elijah is back in Wilkes County recovering from some battle wounds in South Carolina. He is actively recruiting men for the army. He plans to attack next month, and he wants to have an army of 1,000 men when we move out. I will command the Upper Regiment of Richmond County. I know you're in Wilkes County, but your place is right here along the county border, so I thought that I would go ahead and recruit you. I need some good men with fighting experience in my regiment."

Robert stared at the colonel. He was impressed by the man's enthusiasm, but unsure of the reality of his claims. He turned to Frank, who had been sitting quietly and listening to the conversation.

"What do you think, Frank?"

"Why do you care what this slave thinks, Robert? That's the strangest question that I have ever heard," proclaimed Colonel Candler.

"Frank Hammock is not my slave, Colonel," Robert hissed. "He is my neighbor and friend, and an experienced soldier. That scar on the side of his head is from a wound received in the service of the United States. I hold his opinion in very high regard."

The colonel eyed Frank with suspicion and a hint of distrust.

Frank responded, "Well, Mr. Robert, whatever you decide, I'm with you. I'm sure that I don't have many friends or advocates among the Georgia Patriots, but at least none of them have ever beaten me or shot me like the Redcoats and Tories. So if you go, then I'm with you. It's as simple as that."

"I want to go with you, too, Father!" declared Lewis. "I'm old enough to serve this time."

"No, Lewis, you are not old enough to serve in the army. Whether I go or not … I still need you here to take care of the family. And that is my final word. Don't ask me again."

Lewis stomped the ground, crossed his arms, and pouted quietly.

Robert ignored him and paused in anguished thought. He closed his eyes and breathed a short prayer.

"Very well, then, Colonel. If you'll take Frank in the regiment, then I will go, as well. That's my offer."

"Done!" Colonel William Candler shook both of their hands.

The attack upon Augusta was a dismal failure. Though successful at first, the attack lingered into a four-day siege.

On the fourth day British reinforcements arrived from South Carolina. The Patriots of Georgia had to flee for their lives from the British army and attempt to disappear into the backcountry. The British and Tories pursued them and punished them severely.

Governor Wright, the British administrator in Georgia, issued a declaration to his British superiors that called for the complete and utter destruction of the rebels in Georgia. He issued a written declaration:

"The most effectual and best method of crushing the rebellion in the back parts of this country is for an army to march without loss of time into the ceded lands and lay waste and destroy the whole territory."

A British colonel by the name of Cruger set out into the backcountry in search of Colonel Elijah Clarke and his men. He sent patrols in every direction to punish anyone who sympathized with the Patriots. They arrested many people, including old men, women, and children, and marched their prisoners back to the military jail in Augusta. They burned the courthouse in Wilkes County, as well as over one hundred homes and barns. They killed militiamen, plundered farms, burned homes, and drove livestock into the wilderness. The devastation was unspeakable.

Robert and Frank finally made it home safely after the defeat at Augusta. They had to hide in the woods for several days. The two men were starved, exhausted, and discouraged when they rode up to the Hammock home place.

Robert knew that the Hammock family would have to leave Georgia very soon. He had no idea where they might go, but they couldn't stay on their farm. He and his family began making the necessary preparations to leave.

They gathered their possessions, packed food into bags and boxes, loaded supplies into the wagon, and got ready to depart.

The worst possible news arrived on September 23. Davis Mitchell, one of the Patriot militiamen under Colonel Candler, was making the rounds in the vicinity of Wrightsborough to deliver the bad news to the citizens. He galloped into the clearing beside Frank's cabin around mid-morning. He was breathless and his horse was lathered and almost too sick to run.

Robert ran over and grabbed the bridle of the anxious animal. "Davis, what's wrong? Why have you punished your horse like this?"

The young man inhaled deeply and responded with one dry, scratchy word, "Water!"

Lewis and Robert, Jr., arrived almost immediately with two buckets of water. Davis took a long drink and then dumped the rest over his head. Lewis held the other bucket up to the mouth of the exhausted, dehydrated horse.

"The Tories are almost to Wrightsborough!" the man uttered excitedly.

A feeling of terror struck Lewis. He knew what this meant. They were coming after his father!

The messenger continued, "They've issued a decree. The families of all men who joined up with Colonel Clarke and attacked Augusta have to leave Georgia by tomorrow morning or submit to the royal government and take oaths to the king. They promised to hang all men who violated their previous oaths." He paused and stared at Robert. "That includes you. They're coming to hang you, Mr. Robert. And Frank, too. Your names are on their list. You folks have to leave now."

"Are we on our own? Are there others going, as well?" asked Robert.

"Hundreds are fleeing today and heading toward the Savannah River. We'll make our crossing near Dooly's

Fort. But you need to get there by nightfall. We will be leaving the state at first light. You don't want to be left behind."

The young man climbed up on his horse just as Lewis was pouring a fresh bucket of water over the animal's scorched neck.

Robert reached up to shake his hand. "Thank you, Davis. I'll see you at the river."

"Yes, sir. I plan to be there this evening. Pray that I won't get caught by the Tories before then."

"You be careful out there, Davis."

He nodded and spun his horse around, then headed off in a slow trot toward the northwest. He was out of sight in a matter of seconds. Robert turned around and saw the anxious faces of the members of his family. Frank stood with his arm wrapped protectively around Nanye-Hi.

Robert announced, "Well, you heard him. We leave within the hour, ready or not."

Milly and the children waited anxiously near the wagon for Robert to return. He and Frank had left almost an hour before to attend a meeting of Clarke's militia and formulate a plan for the mass exodus and evacuation from Georgia.

The Hammock family had reached the rendezvous site late in the evening and suffered through a restless night's sleep beneath their wagon. Now it seemed like the entire camp, comprised of over seven hundred souls, was preparing to depart immediately. The whole assembly was in an uproar. They were consumed by a generalized state of panic.

The people had a right to be concerned. The arrests and executions were continuing full-force on the frontier. The British overlords wanted blood for the attack upon the city of Augusta, and their Tory servants planned to serve up the heads of the men who served under Elijah Clarke.

At long last Milly caught sight of Robert and Frank approaching from the direction of the headquarters tent. The men were in an obvious hurry. Milly unleashed her verbal concerns the moment that they came within earshot of the wagon.

"I cannot believe this!" proclaimed Milly. "There are hundreds of people encamped here. How will we ever be able to hide such an enormous horde of people in the wilderness?"

"Over seven hundred people, to be precise, my love. And over half of those are women and children. But I don't think that Colonel Clarke has hiding in mind. He wants to move and move fast. We're headed north and west, going all the way over the mountains of North Carolina into the Watauga Settlements."

"North Carolina?" Milly exclaimed in disbelief. "How long will our journey be?"

"About two hundred miles," Robert responded.

Milly didn't respond. She was in such complete shock that she almost stared through Robert. Her face went ashen and she began to tremble.

"Milly, are you all right?" he asked.

Her lip quivered, then she dropped to her knees and began to sob. Her words erupted from her soul in an emotional explosion. "Robert, it's not fair! We've been through so much already. We have fought and killed and run and hidden. All I want is to be left alone and in peace! All I want is a roof over the heads of my children! Is that really so much to ask?"

Robert dropped on one knee beside her and drew her head to his chest, wrapping her in his strong arms. "Now, now, my love. I want that, too. Everyone camped in this field wants the same things that we do. But we cannot have them as long as King George rules us. True peace is only found within freedom, and there is no freedom when tyranny and fear are the weapons of a King."

Lewis and Robbie walked over to their parents. "Papa, we're all loaded and ready to go," Lewis reassured his father. "Mama has gotten everyone fed, packed, and loaded. The little ones are all snug in the wagon. Joshua and John are keeping them busy. The horses are fed and watered. Everything's done. We're just waiting for your word."

Robert looked into his son's deep blue eyes. His look conveyed his pride and satisfaction. "You're a good man, Lewis Hammock. And you too, Robbie. I'm lucky to have such mature, responsible boys. Let's get mounted up and ready to move. Frank will drive the wagon."

"So soon?" asked Milly, wiping the tears from her face.

Robert nodded grimly. "We leave immediately. We'll make our crossing at the low water ford two miles to the west. We'll hold on to our wagon for as long as we can, but sooner or later we will have to go cross-country. When we do we'll most likely have to abandon the rig."

Milly eyed him incredulously. "Robert, we have four very small children. How are they supposed to get to North Carolina without a wagon?"

"They'll walk or ride a horse, just like everyone else."

Milly shook her head in disbelief. "We should never have left Virginia."

"None of that, now!" Robert corrected her. He was growing weary of her complaints. "We look forward, not backward. Everyone out here is in the same predicament that we are. The only way that we're going to survive is to get over those mountains. Now get in the wagon and take care of your children."

He had nothing else to say to her. He turned around and climbed up on his horse. Milly was shocked by her husband's tone. She wasn't accustomed to him speaking to her in such a way. She bit her tongue and climbed up into the rear of the wagon with the little ones.

CHAPTER FOURTEEN
EXODUS

Frank snapped the reins and clucked at the horses. The wagon gave a slight jolt and the wooden frame creaked in protest as it began to move forward with its load of supplies and humans. Frank strained to his left to peer around the rear of the wagon. Just as Robert predicted, the other travelers began to follow them and head west along the river.

Robert pressed onward, completely unaware that he rode at the point of one of the largest mass evacuations of civilian refugees of the American Revolutionary War.

It was a most impressive sight. Hundreds of wayward souls made their way in a wave of humanity that progressed steadily along the wagon trail. There were a handful of wagons like that of the Hammock family's. Many were on horseback. Those who had horses rode on the outer edges of the road.

The vast majority of the travelers were on foot. Hundreds of rifles bristled in the air, carried on the shoulders of the men and boys in the formation. They looked like the quills of a long, skinny porcupine jutting upward toward the sky.

136

They were almost to the river crossing when Colonel Clarke trotted his horse to the head of the column to lead the people across the river. He looked somewhat surprised to see Robert.

"Robert Hammock! I didn't know that you were among our evacuees. I somehow missed seeing you back in camp."

"We arrived late last night, Colonel. I attended the briefing before our departure this morning, but I was standing in the back. I didn't say anything to you ... I knew you were very busy."

"Indeed." He looked at the two boys riding beside Robert. "And who might these young men be?"

"This is my oldest son, Lewis, and my second son, Robert, Jr."

The colonel nodded. "Pleased to meet you, young men. Lewis, you're a handsome, big lad. How old are you, son?"

"I'm fifteen years old, sir."

"Fifteen! Well, then, you're almost old enough to join our cause. What about it? Are you ready to see some action?"

"I've already seen more action over these past couple of years than I would care to describe, Colonel. But I'm willing to do my part, for sure."

The colonel looked curiously at Robert, who simply shook his head and gave the colonel a respectful look that implored, 'Please change the subject.'

The colonel looked back along the enormous convoy of refugees. "Quite an interesting lot behind us, isn't it?"

"Yes, sir."

"Things have changed quite a bit since that glorious day at Kettle Creek, haven't they?"

"Definitely, sir."

"Well, things will change once again, Robert. After we get our families to safety we will return and carry on the fight."

"Carry on the fight? How?" asked Lewis. "The cause is lost in Georgia. There's no more government. There are no more regiments or militia."

Colonel Clarke shook his head. "The Redcoats may control Georgia right now, but our cause is not lost, young man. All we need is one great victory to turn the tide in the South. And we don't need a Georgia government to fight. My men never stopped fighting even after Savannah and Augusta fell.

"We will just be Georgia's Regiment of Refugees ... partisans who live in the wilderness of South Carolina and Georgia and wreak havoc behind enemy lines. Colonel Candler is with us, along with Benjamin Few and several other good officers. We need good men like you, Robert. And you, Lewis. I hope you'll consider returning with us after we get your family to safety over the mountains."

"I'll certainly consider it, Colonel," responded Robert. "But Lewis is going to have to wait."

"I understand. Well, how about we get this mob across the Savannah, shall we?"

He trotted ahead on his horse. The trail reached the river about two hundred yards ahead of the Hammock wagon. They soon joined the colonel by the river's edge.

Clarke stood tall in his saddle and proclaimed to anyone who would listen but no one in particular, "The water is low here. We shall wade across. Stay close and in formation. Watch out for one another, and we'll all make it without incident or loss. Now, Patriots of Georgia, follow me!"

He turned dramatically and trotted into the shallow ford of the Savannah River.

Robert looked to his left and saw his wife's head poking out from beneath the canvas of the wagon. She was staring at the colonel, the look on her face betraying the sarcasm in her heart. She looked at Robert and shook her head in disgust. "I don't see why our very own Moses doesn't whip out his staff and just part the waters for us."

Robert laughed out loud as he led his own horse into the shallow water.

The days of laughter were long gone. After seven hard days on the trail the provisions were running very low. Most of the refugees were not as prepared as Robert and his family. At the rate that they were sharing their foodstuffs the Hammocks would also be running out of necessities very soon. The officers pushed the column very hard. They feared that the enemy in pursuit would soon be upon them.

Their fears were well-founded. General Cornwallis was incensed over the attack upon Augusta. He ordered Major Patrick Ferguson of South Carolina to take his Tory militia and move quickly across the state to cut off Clarke's column before they reached the mountains and put an end to the Georgia rebellion once and for all.

The column of Georgia refugees was in mortal danger. Clarke had no knowledge of the forces that were pursuing him, but he sensed that the enemy was on his heels. He pushed the people mercilessly and urged them northward toward the safety that lay beyond the cloud-shrouded peaks of the Appalachian Mountains of North Carolina.

"It's broken clean through," Frank confirmed. His muffled voice emanated from beneath the wagon that was perched awkwardly in a narrow ditch between two small hills. "The front axle has snapped. There's no fixing it. Even if we were near town, it would have to be replaced by a blacksmith. A repair would take days."

Robert exhaled. "Well, that's it, then. We're on foot or on horseback from here on out. It's a miracle the wagon held out for this long."

"With the ground we've been covering these past three days, I'd say you're right, Mr. Robert. But this rig is not going to move another inch. It's done."

Robert turned to Lewis and Robbie. "Boys, unhitch the team from the wagon and throw a blanket over the horses. We'll rig some simple tethers for them and lead them with our horses. The little ones can ride on them or we can strap on some of our provisions."

"There are no more provisions," snapped Milly. "We used the last of the corn meal last night. All of the dried meat is gone. There's no rice, no wheat, and no corn. That's it."

"Good! Then we won't have to worry about hauling all that stuff," Robert retorted. He was growing weary of his wife's complaints.

"Good? Robert, we haven't had a decent meal for three days, and now there's nothing at all left to eat! We've been moving non-stop for eight days. We need a rest."

"Milly, we have to stay with the group. We have no choice."

"Why? It's not like we're going to lose their trail. After this mob moves through it looks like a herd of bulls has churned up the ground. Besides, we haven't seen another soul since we crossed the Savannah River."

"There are Indians in these woods, Milly. There's probably some of them in the woods up above us who are watching us right now."

She shuddered and stole a quick look into the nearby trees.

"I didn't think of that," she remarked.

"No, I guess you didn't." Robert smiled. "Look, darling, everyone is tired. This column is barely moving, anyway. I'll go up and talk to Colonel Clarke and see what he says."

"Thank you. And I'm sure there are quite a few more wives and mothers in this bunch who will thank you, as well."

Robert smiled kindly at his wife. He then turned and spoke to Frank and the other boys. "I'm going to go see if I can convince the officers to take a rest. But, just in case, get everything we need out of that dead wagon and be ready to move when I get back."

"Yes, sir," Frank and Lewis responded.

Robert climbed slowly into the saddle of his horse. He was thoroughly saddle-sore. His breeches had almost no backside left in them. The cloth had torn and worn away. He also had bleeding blisters on both heels and the sides of his feet. He hated to admit it, but Milly was right. They all needed a rest.

Robert trotted his horse up to the head of the column. He was surprised to discover along the way that a large number of people had already stopped and were scattered about in the woods resting. Some were even building fires.

Robert rode toward his militia commander, Colonel William Candler. The colonel waved at Robert and signaled him to join him and a group of men on horseback near the woods.

"What is going on, Colonel?" Robert inquired.

"Colonel Clarke has called a rest. We're going to go ahead and stop now, even though it is only mid-day, and make camp. We're sending out hunting teams to try and secure some meat. These people need to eat. We can only live off of hickory nuts, paw-paws, and crabapples for so long. People are hungry to the point of mutiny."

"How long are we staying?"

"Right now we're thinking two nights, unless things change. If you would, Robert, please go back down the column and pass the word along. Tell everyone to stop and set up a good camp site. We want everyone to be spread out just a bit for comfort, but close enough for a sound defense."

"Of course, sir. I'll start working my way back down the line."

"Excellent. I or one of my officers will follow up later in the day and check on everyone."

"Yes, sir. And thank you, sir. My wife is going to be very happy."

Colonel Candler grinned. "There will be many happy mothers along this trail tonight … if we can get their children fed. Now get going. Spread the good news."

Robert flashed an awkward salute and spun his horse around. As he meandered among the throng of travelers he informed everyone he could about the two-night respite. The good news traveled fast. It almost beat him back to his family's place among the exiles.

Robert grew more excited as he neared his wagon. He was anxious to deliver the news to his wife. He jumped off of the horse as if he were a young man again and grabbed his wife in an embrace. He spun her around in a circle, dancing a makeshift celebration in the forest.

"Heavens be, Robert Hammock! What has gotten into you?"

"Just a little good news, my love." He kissed her smartly on the lips and then called over his shoulder, "Boys, cut that canvas off of the wagon! We need us a good tent shelter for the next couple of nights."

"Couple of nights?" Milly asked in disbelief.

"Yes ma'am. Colonel Clarke has called a halt. We are camping here for two nights and foraging for provisions." He winked at Frank. "Frank, are you ready to try some hunting?"

"Oh, yes sir!"

"You and Lewis take to the woods. Stay together, though. We're mighty close to Cherokee country."

"Why can't I go?" Robbie wailed.

"Because I need you here to help set up camp, son. You can go tomorrow, though, and Lewis can stay back in camp."

"Yes, sir," Robbie conceded grudgingly.

"All right, let's get to work, Hammock family! This is our home for the next two days."

"Shh! Did you hear that?" Frank cocked his head to the right as he listened intently in the direction of the hillside. He and Lewis were seated quietly in a makeshift blind close to a deer trail. About an hour after leaving the camp in search of game they discovered the trail that led down to a partially dry creek. There were two deep pools that still held water and numerous deer tracks leading to both pools. They had already bagged three squirrels and a raccoon, but they decided to hide and see if they might get lucky and see a deer.

Lewis listened intently. "I don't hear anything."

"I could have sworn that I heard something up the hill."

They sat quietly in their well-covered hideout. Frank focused intently on the deer trail and ridge line. Lewis, however, was becoming quite bored. He began to amuse himself by inventing a game of herding ants that were busily entering and exiting a nearby anthill. Suddenly a rather large crashing sound carried down the hillside. Lewis grabbed his rifle and aimed it in the direction of the sound.

"Now I know you heard that!" whispered Frank.

"What was it? It sounded huge!"

Frank shook his head subtly. "I hope it's a deer. Could be a man. Keep a sharp eye out."

They each peered down the barrels of their weapons and watched the line where the dark floor of the forest met the bright sky beyond the ridge. Suddenly a huge shadow appeared over the hill. It was moving directly toward them!

"Good God, what is that? Is it a buffalo? Or is it a bear?" Lewis hissed, trembling.

"I can't tell yet. Be still and quiet. Might be a bear, or an elk. They have elk up here in the hills."

"It's coming this way, whatever it is," observed Lewis.

The huge beast continued on a straight line down the hill toward their position. Frank reached forward and gently pulled back the hammer on his musket. It responded with a subtle, hollow click. He was just about to fire his weapon when the animal gave its loud, deep, terrifying call.

"Moooooo ...."

Then the rather large brown and white cow wandered up to the spot where they were hiding and hung its head over the top of their blind. The cow licked the top of Frank's cocked hat.

Lewis looked incredulously at Frank. "There is no way that just happened."

Dozens of mouths hung open in disbelief when Frank and Lewis emerged from the woods with a cow in tow. Lewis led the animal by the short length of rope that dangled from its neck. It had obviously been tied up at a farm or homestead somewhere nearby but had managed to escape. It seemed genuinely happy to come upon human beings in the woods. Of course, the condemned animal had no idea of the fate that awaited it back at the refugee camp.

Milly saw them coming from a distance down the trail. She called over her shoulder to her husband. She greeted them with both of her fists planted firmly on her hips. Robert greeted them with a huge smile.

"Boys, where in heaven's name did you get that cow? Please tell me you didn't steal it."

"No, ma'am. It just wandered up to us while we were set up on a deer trail about a quarter mile west of here," Lewis testified.

She eyed her husband with a dubious look. "So what you're telling me is that a cow ... this cow ... just walked up to you in the woods, with rope dangling from its neck, and invited you to haul it back to this encampment?"

Lewis grinned and replied, "Yes ma'am."

Her gaze shifted to Frank.

"It's the gospel truth, Miss Milly. We thought it was a buffalo or a bear at first until we heard it bellow. The stupid animal walked right up to the spot where we were hiding as if it knew we would be there. Lewis just grabbed the rope and then we headed on back."

"So you didn't steal that cow?" she confirmed.

"No ma'am, we found the cow. Or, should I say, she found us," Frank reassured Milly.

Robert shook his head and chuckled. "Did you gentlemen happen to get anything else?"

"A few squirrels and a big coon," answered Lewis.

"Well, just go ahead and give those away to whoever will take them. We've got beef to prepare! That beast should feed a fair portion of this camp tonight. Robbie, fetch my skinning knife!"

Robert, Frank, and the boys soon set about the gruesome but necessary task of slaughtering the cow. A crowd gathered quickly. The people were hungry. It appeared that things might get out of control without some military leadership. Once the animal was down and skinned, Robert sent Lewis ahead to fetch one of the officers and inform them of the situation.

Ten minutes later Colonel Clarke and two of his captains, along with about ten other militiamen, made their way from the head of the group.

"Squire Lewis tells me that you might need a little help with meat distribution back here at the Hammock butcher shop." Colonel Clarke was grinning broadly.

"Yes, sir. The boys stumbled upon a cow running loose in the woods and brought it back to camp. We'd like to keep several pounds of the choice cuts for our family. But after that I don't want any part of seeing who gets the rest. I'd be mighty grateful if you and your men would distribute the meat."

The colonel nodded. "That sounds fair enough. It's your kill. You gentlemen take your cut and we'll take care of the rest for you, Robert. This meat won't feed everyone, but it will help. Two of the lads up ahead each got a deer off to the east, and there's been a fair bit of small game taken. We should be able to get a reasonable meal for everyone by nightfall."

Robert quickly and skillfully removed the portions or meat that he wanted and then turned over the rest to the colonel. Nothing went to waste. The hungry travelers claimed all of the cuts, as well as the organs, brain, intestines, and tongue. Before it was over people even took ownership of the bones, which were boiled into a thin soup. The starving wanderers cracked open the bones and scraped out the marrow to flavor the broth.

Over and over again, around all of the campfires that night, the story was told of Lewis Hammock and the Negro named Frank who found a cow wandering in the woods. It quickly became a camp legend as less-than-accurate details were added to the tale.

Seven days later the starving band of exiles stumbled into the Watauga Valley. They were welcomed into the arms and homes of unimaginably generous mountain folk. Everything was prepared for their arrival. Their humble hosts fed them, clothed them, and shared their homes with them. It was an oasis of generosity and grace in the midst of a savage war.

The Hammock family, because it was larger than most of the families in the group, was offered the use of a small warehouse for their shelter. It wasn't much of a warehouse, really. It was merely a rough, older cabin that had been used for community storage. But it was a dry space and provided adequate protection from the cold mountain air. It was the first week of October, and the nights had taken on a chill.

As night fell several women stopped by their cabin and left food items for the family. One particularly filthy, but generous, mountain man appeared with two large bear skins and an elk skin. Robert spread the furry hides over the floor as a cushion for his family. They provided a soft, warm barrier against the cold of the earth beneath.

Milly and Nanye-Hi prepared and fed the family a quick makeshift meal and then everyone collapsed from exhaustion. No one bothered to remove their coats, breeches, or even their weskits. They slept fully clothed. As Robert slipped into unconsciousness he wondered if he would ever see his home in Georgia again.

CHAPTER FIFTEEN
MOUNTAIN AMBUSH

The Georgians gathered in the clearing in the center of the village. There were almost eighty fighting men, fully equipped and ready to mount their horses. They were all saying their final farewells to loved ones and friends. It was a deeply moving time. Though no one would speak about it, many realized that this could be the last time that they might ever see their wives and children.

Robert enjoyed the attention of his little congregation of Hammock children. He was down on one knee and hugging all of the little ones at once. His eyes caught the concerned stare of his son, Lewis. Robert stood up and walked over to his handsome teenage son.

"Lewis, I'm counting on you to watch over the family while I'm gone. It's a lot of responsibility."

"Yes, Father. I know what is expected of me."

"You'll need to hunt and work and do all of the things that I would do if I were here."

"Yes, Father. I know." He paused and stared at the ground dejectedly. "But I sure wish that I was going with you."

"I know you do, son. But you're needed here."

148

"I know ... to haul water and take care of the family."

Robert shook his head. "Not just that. I've already informed Colonel Sevier that you are staying behind. He fully expects you to perform your share of service in the militia. You will have to serve guard duty and go on patrols, just like all of the other men in the settlements."

Lewis's eyes lit up. "Really, Father? Is that true?"

"Absolutely, son. They need good, responsible fighting men. I assured the colonel that you would be a valuable contributor to the defense of the settlements."

Lewis stuck out his hand. "Thank you, sir. I'll do my duty."

Robert pushed his hand away good-naturedly and grabbed his son, pulling him close for a hug. The other boys piled on for a group hug. Milly watched the entire event unfold with tears of joy mixed with sorrow.

Robert tore himself away from the boys and gave his full attention to Milly.

"I'll be back as soon as I can."

"You'd better. I'll be expecting you back here as soon as the job is done. Give Cornwallis a little piece of lead from me." She jumped into his arms and wrapped her own arms around his neck. As he held her close she whispered into his ear, "I'll be waiting for you to come back to me."

Robert hugged her even closer.

On the other side of the clearing Frank knelt before his children. Anna toddled about on the ground, completely unaware of the events unfolding before her eyes. Simeon, now almost three years old, understood that something important was happening. The tears in his father's eyes disturbed him.

The little boy cupped his hand beneath Frank's chin. "Why you cry, Papa?"

Frank wiped his nose and smiled at his boy. "I have to go away for a while, Simeon. I am going to miss you and your mama and sister."

"Why you go?" he asked innocently.

"I must go and make things better so we can go back home."

"Back to Georgia!" The youngster announced. He had no idea what Georgia was, but he heard the people around him talk about it all of the time.

"Yes, Simeon. Back to our cabin in Georgia."

"You come back soon?" the little boy asked, a tear forming in his eye.

"As soon as I can, son."

Frank wrapped the little boy in his arms and hugged him close. He looked up into the gorgeous, dark eyes of his bride. They were puffy and stained with tears. Frank stood and wrapped his arms around her.

"Please take care of yourself, husband," she pleaded. "I almost lost you once already. I cannot bear thinking of my life without you."

"I will come back to you, my Cherokee beauty." He smiled broadly.

"We will be waiting for you when you return," she promised. "All four of us."

Frank's head jerked backwards in confusion. "All four of us?"

Nanye-Hi patted her belly. "There will be another coming in the late spring. Another arrow for your quiver." She grinned.

Frank roared an emotional cry, causing dozens of people nearby to turn their heads and stare in confusion. Some looked with haughty, judgmental eyes at the black man and his Indian wife with their half-breed children. But Frank and Nanye-Hi did not care. He picked up his wife in his strong arms and hugged her tight.

"I love you, Nanye-Hi."

"And I love you, my husband."

Minutes later the men were mounted and heading toward British-controlled South Carolina.

Lewis Hammock had a new friend. The young man's name was Patrick Hix. The boys were about the same age and had become almost instant pals. After several weeks together they were practically inseparable.

Patrick had lived in the mountains since he was a small boy, and he took great joy in teaching Lewis all of the strategies and tricks of successful mountain life and hunting. The militia officers saw how well the boys complemented one another, so they began scheduling them together on guard duty and patrols.

It was early December. The boys were riding toward the south on an extended patrol in search of possible Indian encroachment. A rumor had reached the village the day prior about a raid upon a remote trading post down in that direction, at the edge of the Cherokee lands. Colonel Sevier had dispatched four patrols to fan out and look for any sign of Cherokee.

The boys had been riding for a little over an hour and were following a game trail just below the crest of a wide ridge when Patrick raised his fist and called a sudden stop. He lifted his finger to his lips and then pointed down toward the ground beside the trail.

Patrick jumped silently from his horse and Lewis followed suit. The boys tip-toed to the edge of the trail and knelt down. Patrick pointed at a tiny broken limb.

"There's sign here of fresh riders," he whispered. "This here limb's been broke."

He pointed also to the mixture of tracks in front of their horses.

"I've been noticin' pony tracks amongst the deer, elk, and bear. Ponies is on top. That means Injuns done passed since the last rain. More'n likely yestiddy afternoon or early this mornin'. We need to keep our eyes and ears open."

Lewis nodded his understanding. "We're a long way from the settlements."

"A fer piece, sure 'nough," agreed Patrick. "Prob'ly too fer to be safe. I've been a mite stupid. We need to start makin' our way back. Let's keep it slow, easy, and quiet. Colonel Sevier needs to know about this."

The boys mounted their horses and quickly turned them around on the trail and pointed them back toward home. They had gone less than a quarter of a mile when Patrick signaled for another stop.

"What's the matter?" asked Lewis.

Patrick sniffed the air. "Did you smell that?"

"All I smell is that dead coon we saw a while back. It's still burned into my nose," Lewis quipped.

Patrick shook his head. He obviously thought that it was no time for jokes.

"No, I caught me a whiff of somethin' differ'nt. Sumpin' smoky. Like a man scent. It was just a tiny whiff, but I know I smelt it. Let's get movin'. Somethin' don't feel right."

The boys gently kicked their horses, urging them to resume their journey northward along the trail. Patrick rode in the front, with Lewis only ten feet behind. Patrick picked up his pace noticeably, so Lewis did the same. They soon approached a narrow draw between two huge tree-covered rocks. Eons of water flow had made the cut on the mountainside, forming a perfect funnel through rock for the game trail. It was just wide enough for a horse to pass through.

Lewis never saw what alerted Patrick, but suddenly the boy leaned forward over the neck of his horse and screamed, "Ambush!" His high-pitched voice shattered the serene silence of the forest. He kicked vigorously at the sides of his horse, prodding the animal into a run, and heading straight toward the cut in the rock.

The next sound that punctured the tranquility of the Carolina woods was the crack of a rifle. The first shot was followed by several more. Lead slammed into the rock that surrounded the boys. Lewis felt the sting of the dust and rock fragments against the skin of his face and hands. He heard the dull thud of metal impacting meat and saw Patrick's horse gave a brief lurch, but the animal kept moving forward.

The boys were in the narrow, crowded draw between the boulders when the arrows began to rain down upon them. Lewis glanced up and saw several Indians at the top of the western side of the draw. Most of their arrows bounced harmlessly off of the stone walls that surrounded them. But some found their mark. He saw an arrow protruding from the rump of Patrick's horse.

Up ahead of him Patrick screamed in pain. Lewis could not see how badly he was hurt. Lewis winced at a searing pain in his arm just above the left wrist. Then he realized that he couldn't even move his arm! He looked down in horror to see that an arrow had penetrated the flesh of his forearm and imbedded into the pommel of his saddle. His horse whinnied almost to the point of screaming. He had never heard such a sound out of a horse before. Surely an arrow or bullet had struck his horse, as well!

Then Lewis felt a scorching fire in his back. His injury was mid-way down and near his left side. He reached back awkwardly with his right hand and felt the shaft of an arrow protruding from his hunting frock. Something beyond fear gripped him. It was the sudden realization that he might very well die on that mountainside ... that he might never see his mother or his family again.

At long last they emerged from the narrow rock canyon onto the open trail beyond.

"We're almost clear!" wailed Patrick, his voice betraying the pain in his body. "We have to get around that bend and behind the hill! Forty more yards!"

They were now well outside of the range of the bows, but the rifle fire quickly resumed. Lead slammed into trees, ricocheted off of rocks, and threw clouds of leaves and mud into the air.

Lewis screamed, "God, Almighty, how many of them are there?"

"I don't know. It don't matter. We have to keep moving!"

Just before rounding that final bend a bullet screamed past Lewis's ear. It must have been only inches away. He felt the vibration of the air that it displaced as it flew past him. The bullet struck Patrick with a loud and distinct 'whack.' He lurched forward across the pommel of his saddle and hung awkwardly across his horse's neck. Without Patrick's urging, the horse slowed down to almost a complete stop.

There was neither the time nor the opportunity to stop and asses his friends injuries. The projectiles continued to fly over the hilltop. The Indians were less that a hundred yards behind them and certain to pursue. Lewis burst past Patrick on the trail, grabbed the fallen reins of his friend's horse, and pulled the animal along the trail in the direction of the settlements.

Lewis awakened with a throbbing headache. He wasn't sure where he was or how he got there. He blinked his eyes in an effort to focus his vision. Then he heard the familiar voices of his family. He was back at his temporary home in the Watauga Valley. He was alive … and safe.

Robbie's voice called across the room, "Mama, he's awake! Lewis is awake!"

A crowd of brothers and sisters descended upon him. Robbie, Josh, and John just stood and smiled. Elizabeth, Nancy, Lucy, little Daniel Chandler, Simeon, and Anna all attempted to crawl onto the bed with Lewis and shower him with hugs and kisses.

"All right, you little ones, off you go!" scolded Milly. "Lewis doesn't need you crawling all over him like maggots on a carcass. Now shoo! Go and play."

The children scurried outside into the cool December morning. Only Robbie remained inside with his mother. Lewis heard movement by the fireplace and caught a quick glance of Nanye-Hi as she was tending to a cooking pot.

"What happened, Mama?"

"What happened? Land sakes, boy! You were shot to pieces by Indian arrows, that's what happened! Don't you remember?"

"I remember the ambush and getting hit by a couple of arrows. I remember riding toward home and guiding Patrick's horse after he got hit." He paused and his eyes registered a flood of memories coming back to him. He tried to sit up, but the pain in his side drew him back down onto the bed. "Where is Patrick? How is he doing?"

Milly took him by the hand and looked gently into his eyes. "Son, Patrick is dead."

Lewis felt the tears welling up in his eyes. Ashamed, he dropped back down onto the bed and threw his unwounded arm up over his face. He did not want his mother to see his emotions on display.

Milly patted him on the leg. "Now, now, son. It's all right to be upset about your friend. You have nothing to be ashamed of. Patrick was a fine friend to you, and you ought to mourn his passing."

Lewis attempted to wipe the tears from his eyes. "When did he die?"

"Lewis, he was dead long before you even arrived here. And from what we could tell you had been unconscious for a while, yourself. The horses simply followed the trail back home."

"How's my horse?"

"Just fine. She had a pretty big cut on the hip. Mr. Andrews said it was from an arrow. But it was superficial. It's been cleaned and cared for. She'll be fine and ready to ride again in no time. Patrick's horse was a mess, though. That poor gelding had been hit twice by rifle fire and had an arrow in its rump and still managed to make it home. But it was beyond hope. They had to put the poor animal down."

"How long have I been asleep?"

"Two days," chimed in Robbie. "Mama said you had a little bit of fever the first night, but you've just been sleeping for the most part."

"Am I hurt bad? I feel a little sore, but I don't feel all that bad."

"The arrow in your forearm went right between the two bones," explained Robbie. "The head stuck in your saddle. They think that's what helped keep you balanced on your horse the whole way back. They had to break the arrow just to get you down."

Lewis looked at the tight bandage around his left arm. He felt tenderness in his side in the front as well as in the back. He looked under his shirt and saw a spot of blood on the bandage that was wrapped around his waist.

"What is this blood from in the front? I remember feeling the arrow sticking out of the back on that side, but it's sore in the front, as well."

Milly responded, "Well, son, that arrow was tough to get out. It was imbedded in that muscle in your side, not deep enough to get into you guts or organs. But those horrible arrows have such nasty barbs on them. They couldn't back the arrow out, so they had to push it on through and out the front. Once the head was broken off, they pulled the shaft out."

Lewis's eyes grew wide in disbelief.

Milly grinned and tousled his hair. "I know it sounds horrible, but these mountain men know what they're doing. All in all it was a pretty superficial wound. You lost a little blood, but you'll be just fine. Like Robbie said, you had a touch of fever that first night, but you're a strong lad. Your body has healed nicely. You'll be up and about in a couple more days." She nodded toward Robert, Jr. "Your brother has been doing a fine job of taking care of things while you've been down. I'm blessed to have raised such fine young men."

Lewis noticed a bruise and bloody scratches on Robert's right temple.

"What happened to you, Robbie?"

"I had a little accident the day you got hurt. Had me a run-in with a tree limb while I was hunting nuts with Nanye-Hi. I'm fine. She patched me up while everybody else was taking care of you."

Nanye-Hi walked over to where Lewis lay. She observed, "You must be hungry. Would you like some soup?"

"Oh, yes. Very much!"

She smiled broadly. "I will get you some."

Nanye-Hi was diverted from her soup preparation by a loud banging on the cabin door. She was closest to the door, so she opened it. A stout, burly mountain resident was standing outside. He was fully armed with blades and flintlocks.

"Is Mrs. Hammock in?" he asked harshly.

"I'm right here." Milly crossed the room to greet their guest.

"Ma'am. I'm Andrew Joslin. The colonel has asked me to pass the word along ... you folks need to stay in close to the settlement until further notice. No one is to leave the area without say-so from the colonel."

"Why, Mr. Joslin? What is wrong?"

"The Cherokees are upon us. They're threatenin' the valley."

"Oh, my Lord! What has happened?"

"A patrol found old Abner Faris less than a quarter mile to the west. He was shot and scalped. The critters have done worked him over, too."

The Hammock children all gazed fearfully at their mother.

"The colonel's affeared that an attack is comin', so you folks mind his orders and stay in your home." He looked angrily at Nanye-Hi. "Especially your Injun girl. It ain't safe for her to be out and about. We don't want no one gettin' shot by accident, iff'n you know what I mean."

CHAPTER SIXTEEN
LEWIS THE LEGEND

Lewis and Robbie had been gone for most of the morning. Milly was beginning to get worried. The cabin door flew open just as her motherly instincts were guiding her mind toward all manner of tragedies that might have befallen her sons. The sudden blast of winter wind brought a chorus of griping from inside the warm cabin. Lewis and Robbie walked in quickly from the cold and began kicking the snow off of their shoes and leggings.

Milly and Nanye-Hi descended upon the boys and began to peel the layers of protective buckskin and wool off of their frozen bodies.

"Did you see any sign?" asked Milly.

Lewis frowned and shook his head. "No, Mother. Not a thing. All I saw were the footprints of men who have been out hunting like us. But no sign of deer. Nothing at all. The critters are smart, I guess. They're all probably laid up in a dry, sheltered crag in these mountains. Or maybe they've been hunted out. I don't know. We might not see any sign until some of this snow melts off."

159

She spoke reassuringly, "Well, at least you tried. Some fresh meat would have been nice, but we'll be all right."

"There's just nothing out there, Mother. No rabbits, no turkeys. We didn't even see a squirrel," muttered Robbie in disbelief.

"Well, like Lewis said, things will get better when the snow lets up a bit. It can't stay this cold forever. Meanwhile, let's get those shoes off and get some hot food in you right now. We have a hot stew and corn cakes. Nanye-Hi will add a squirt of rum to your tea to help warm you up."

A few minutes later the boys were seated in front of the fire and wrapped in warm wool blankets, enjoying a hot bowl of salty, tasty stew made from smoked pork and brown beans. The hot food and fire did much to chase the cold from their bones.

Winter had descended with a fury upon the mountains. December was unusually cold, but by the first week of January the air was frigid. And then the snows began. The winter weather systems moved through every three or four days, dumping one coating after another of dry, powdery snow. By January 15 there was well over two feet of the fluffy white ice on the ground.

The residents and refugees in the Watauga settlements holed up in their cabins, burned their ample supplies of firewood, and attempted to stay warm. Meanwhile, they all prayed that their food supplies would hold out.

The one good thing about the snow and winter weather was the guaranteed absence of Indians. No one was moving about in this harsh weather ... not even the natives.

So the Hammock family hunkered down like all of the other local residents and survived on their reserves. In the fall there had been the occasional gift of food from local families, but once the winter set in such generosity had become quite scarce. It wasn't that the local people didn't want to help the refugees. It was simply a matter of limited resources and lack of supply. Every family and household was actively struggling for survival.

Truth be told, most of the locals considered Lewis to be quite capable of providing for the Hammock family. The young man had become something of a local legend since surviving the Indian attack and returning over ten miles both in a semi-conscious state and pinned to his saddle by a Cherokee arrow. Young and old alike, people looked up to Lewis. Even though he was not yet sixteen years old the men of the village treated him like a man. He performed his duty on patrol just like the others.

But as rewarding as all of that respect and "adult" treatment were to Lewis, he would trade it all for a nice, fat doe. His family was rapidly growing weary of salted pork from barrels, musty corn meal, and shriveled potatoes.

After the boys ate the meager meal they both leaned back-to-back against one another. Lewis asked his mother for his deer antler pipe and tobacco. She fetched the items for him without complaint. She had raised an eyebrow the first time Lewis fired up his pipe while sitting in front of the fireplace. But then she figured that if he was old enough to go on patrols and fight Indians, that he was certainly old enough to enjoy a pipe if he wanted to.

Lewis crumbled some of his father's tobacco into the generous bowl of the pipe, grabbed a coal with his tongs, and drew in the sweet smoke. His homemade pipe burned extremely well. He had modeled it after the one that was carried by his old friend Wappanakuk. Lewis leaned back against Robbie and they were soon wrapped in a fog of tobacco smoke.

"Boy, does that smell remind me of Papa," remarked Robbie.

"Yep," affirmed Lewis.

They sat in silence for a moment.

Robbie sighed. "I wonder where Papa is right now. And Frank, too. I hope they're as warm and well-fed as we are right now."

Lewis weighed his words for a moment, and then said, "I just hope that they're both still alive."

Robert Hammock was guarding British prisoners. The Patriot forces had just won an amazing victory at Cowpens, South Carolina. The British forces were utterly defeated. One hundred and fifty Redcoats died in the battle and almost seven hundred more were captured by the American army. So Robert was on prisoner duty. And there were a lot of prisoners!

It was hard for him to really enjoy the victory because his loyal friend, Frank, was gone ... forever. The former slave died in a battle at Long Cane over a month before. Frank had actually been pulling their commander, Colonel Elijah Clarke, to safety when he was struck by the fatal bullet. He died in Robert's arms. He died a free man. Robert buried the young man alongside the thirteen other Patriots who perished in the same battle.

Yes, it was a great victory, but all Robert really wanted to do was go home to his family. Even a temporary home in the mountains would be nice. He desperately wanted to see his wife and children. And he needed to deliver the news of Frank's death to Nanye-Hi and the children.

Robert was keeping watch over the prisoners entrusted to him and listening to a rather colorful argument ongoing among some of the junior officers of his regiment when he heard someone call his name.

"Robert Hammock! Is that you?"

Robert turned and discovered an Indian on horseback approaching him from the center of the battlefield. Robert's jaw dropped in disbelief.

His lips formed a single word ... "Wappanakuk!"

Wappanakuk jumped down from his horse and the two men embraced, both of them grinning from ear to ear.

Patriot militiamen and British prisoners alike stared out of curiosity.

"What in heaven's name are you doing here?" Robert exclaimed.

"I have been serving as a scout for the North Carolina State Dragoons. They have a small contingent of about thirty men here."

"But why are you involved in this war? I never imagined that you would ever take up arms for either side."

Wappanakuk frowned and his face became tense and stormy in appearance. He took a deep breath and weighed his response.

"Robert, a British patrol entered our village two years ago. They killed two young men because they dared to walk out of their homes with weapons. They accused us of being rebels against King George and then confiscated our livestock and burned our crops. One of their soldiers harmed a young woman of our village ... my sister."

"Good Lord! I am so sorry, old friend."

"So, as you see now, I was forced to choose a side. I fight against those who would attack and disarm my people. And, besides, I have a couple of good friends fighting for the American cause." He smiled broadly. "But why are you alone?" He scanned the field near Robert. "Where is Frank?"

Robert frowned and shook his head. "Frank fell in the battle at Long Cane last month, along with thirteen other good men."

"Oh, Robert, I am so sorry to learn of this. Frank was a good fellow ... a fine young man. I considered him to be a good friend."

"Indeed he was. I have missed him greatly." Robert paused. "You know ... I gave him his freedom papers back last year. He died a free man."

"That is commendable, Robert. But not unexpected. I could see the way that you cared for the boy. He may have been a slave on paper, but clearly he was not so in the hearts of the members of your family. It was only a matter of time."

"He was planning to stay with us in Georgia. I deeded him one hundred and fifty acres of land, and he was planning to make his home beside mine."

Wappanakuk placed his hand on Robert's shoulder. "Again, just as I expected he would. He cared for you very deeply, Robert. He told me so."

Robert took a deep, cleansing breath. "I just dread the day that I have to return and tell his wife about his death in battle."

"So, Frank had a wife. That is good."

"Oh, I forgot! You left us before he was married. You met his wife in Georgia."

"I did?"

Frank nodded and grinned. "He married the Indian girl, Nanye-Hi ... the one we discovered in the woods."

Wappanakuk laughed out loud. "Of course! I should have known! I saw the romance between them."

Robert nodded his head. "She was a wonderful wife to him. They were very good for one another. She has borne him two children and is expecting another in the spring."

"So tragic. Yet it is a story that is becoming all too common in these violent times. Many children will grow up in America without their fathers. Many wives will mourn their husbands, dead and buried on distant battlefields."

"Indeed. I have seen far too much death, my friend, as have my wife and children. But, of course, you already know all about that."

Wappanakuk nodded silently. "Robert, I must admit that I am surprised to see you here fighting in South Carolina. Aren't the British still in control in Georgia? Who is caring for Milly and the children?"

Robert opened his eyes wide and shook his head. "Oh, they are not in Georgia. Not anymore."

"No? Where are they?"

"I took them into the mountains of North Carolina, into the place called Watauga. After we besieged Augusta last year and failed to take the city a Tory colonel by the name of Brown unleashed his fury on the Georgia backcountry. The Loyalists began to arrest, imprison, and kill Whigs and their family members. They were destroying homes and property. So we fled. We had no other choice. The British had a warrant out for me and all of the other men who had attacked Augusta."

Robert continued, "Colonel Elijah Clarke took us on a great trek through the mountains. Over seven hundred pilgrims, many of them women and children, walked over two hundred miles. It was a sight to behold."

"So do you plan to live there? Will that be your new home?"

"I pray not. We want to go back home to the Georgia backcountry, but the British and their Tory allies must be driven from Augusta first."

"Perhaps it will not be long now. I sense that the fortunes of this war are turning. The British control much less land here in South Carolina now. After today's tremendous victory, who knows what might happen in this war?"

The Refugees of Georgia departed with Colonel Pickens' army and established camp four miles to the west of the battlefield on the banks of Little Buck Creek. Wappanakuk went with them, as well. He sought and received his release from the North Carolina Militia in order to join Robert in the Georgia camp. There were also several dozen of the Overmountain Men with them. Most of those men were veterans of the great victory at King's Mountain. They were all aching to return to their homes.

A full week of boring camp life passed. It was February 1, 1781. The weather turned cold and wet. So far it had been only a cold rain, but the men feared the coming of ice and snow. The militia army had no orders to move and were on the verge of building shacks and, much to the disappointment of the men, move into a full-fledged winter camp.

Quite unexpectedly Major John Cunningham, the temporary commander of the regiment during Colonel Clarke's recovery from wounds and sickness, was summoned to Colonel Pickens' tent for a briefing. He returned one hour later with a skip in his step and a broad smile on his face.

"Gentlemen, gather around. I have good news!"

It took several minutes for the eighty men of the regiment to assemble around their commander. They could see the excitement in Major Cunningham's eyes. His good mood became infections among the men. Robert sat on the ground near the front of the assembly. Wappanakuk sat by his side. The men all chatted excitedly.

Major Cunningham attempted to calm the crowd. "Boys, be quiet now! Listen up! I have a wonderful announcement to make."

A rapid hush descended upon the gathering.

"Colonel Pickens is disbanding the militia for a time of furlough. We are being released until March 15, when he requests that we rejoin him at his plantation in the Long Cane District."

"That's six weeks from now, Major. What do we do in the meantime? Where do we go?" asked one of the soldiers.

"You can go wherever you please. You can stay here in winter camp, though I doubt that many will want to do that. You can attach yourself to another militia outfit or maybe scout for the Continentals. You can go back to Georgia, but I would advise against that. Brown has warrants out for all of us. Personally, I am going to Watauga to visit with my family. If you have loved ones in the mountains I recommend that you do the same."

The men erupted with excitement. It was clear that most of them planned to head for the mountains.

"You men are free to leave as you wish. It's a little late in the day for me. I'm remaining here tonight and leaving at first light tomorrow. You are all welcome to join me. I believe that we will be safer traveling together. The mountain soldiers are leaving in the morning, as well."

The men stared at him with a mixture of excitement and disbelief.

"Well, that's it, gentlemen. That's all I have. Go and prepare yourselves for travel. Dress warmly and scrounge up all of the food that you can. We have a few days' ride coming and some pretty tough ground to cover. Behave yourselves tonight, and I'll see you bright and early in the morning."

Robert leaned toward Wappanakuk. "How would you like to spend a little time in the mountains?"

"I was hoping that you would ask," he responded.

The men riding toward the Watauga settlements were an imposing force, indeed. There were one hundred and thirty of them, all armed and on horseback. The seasoned horsemen traversed the creeks and mountain draws with ease. They were making excellent time in their quest to reach their families beyond the mountains.

By the second night of travel they were encamped in the low mountains of North Carolina, just above the snow line. Despite the frigid cold and snow there was a spirit of anticipation in the camp. The Refugees had not seen their families for several months. The men of Watauga, though they had only been gone for a few weeks in response to the call-up for Cowpens, were just as eager to return to their mountain homes.

The soldiers rested on that second night beside raging campfires. They cut pine limbs and created a thick layer of the soft needles between their backsides and the six inches of snow that coated the ground. They greatly enjoyed the quiet and peace of the mountains.

Robert and Wappanakuk traded rum, tobacco, and stories with several of the Watauga men. One of those men, quite full of the rum, listened intently to Robert's story about meeting Wappanakuk on the King's Highway seven years prior.

The drunken mountain man proclaimed, "I like you, pilgrim! You tell good stories. What's your name, Georgia boy?"

"My name is Robert Hammock."

"Hammock?" the man exclaimed. "You ain't no kin to the legendary Lewis Hammock, ere ya?"

Robert's face registered confusion. "Why, yes, I have a son named Lewis Hammock. He is my oldest son."

The man belched loudly. "You talkin' 'bout Lewis Hammock up in Watauga with his mama and that Injun girl and all them little brothers and sisters?"

Robert nodded nervously. "Yes, that is my Lewis Hammock ... and that is my family."

The man slapped him on the shoulder. "Well, I tell you what! I am mighty proud to meet you! That Lewis Hammock is one tough little feller! He went up agin' a whole war party of Cherokee with just one other boy with him. Got all shot to pieces full of lead and arrows and still made it back to the valley with his dead buddy and both of their hosses. That little cuss was flat-out nailed to his saddle! Had an arrow clear through the arm and right into the saddle leather. I ain't ever seen or heerd of nothin' else like it!"

Robert's breathing increased and his face flushed. His mind raced. Surely this man wasn't talking about his son!

Surely his son had not faced down a Cherokee war party! And the drunken mountain man left out the most important part. Did Lewis survive?

Robert blurted out, "But he's alive, right? You're telling me that Lewis Hammock is alive? That he is well?"

"Alive?" responded the drunk, confused mountain man. He tossed back another gulp of rum. "Yeah, he's alive! That's for sure! Tough kid, that one. And he's your son, you say? Well, you should be plenty proud. He's all grit and fight, that little Lewis Hammock. Every soul in Watauga is safe with that boy ridin' patrol in them hills."

Robert cast an anxious glance at Wappanakuk, who smiled at him with eyebrows raised. His only response was, "That's our Tarowa Yetashta ... our Little Warrior."

CHAPTER SEVENTEEN
QUIET DAYS IN THE MOUNTAINS

Lewis gently rubbed the wound on his side. It did not hurt that much. Mostly he felt a dull ache, especially when it was cold. And this was a particularly cold morning. But at least it was a quiet morning. There had not been any sign of Cherokee raiders for the past few weeks. The elders believed that the natives were still laying low in their winter encampments to the south.

Lewis enjoyed the peace and quiet. He particularly enjoyed his solo missions as a scout and Indian spy. Ever since his best friend, Patrick, died, he was reluctant to get close to anyone else or make any new friends. He had become something of a loner ... which was fine on any ordinary day. But it could definitely be a problem if he encountered any trouble in the wilderness.

Lewis sighed and mumbled almost silently to himself, "I reckon I need to bring Robbie with me next time. He needs to learn about scouting and soldiering, anyway."

He scanned the nearby hillsides for any sign of threat or movement. He caught the brief flash of white   from the tail of a deer as it darted over the hillside to his left. Lewis guided his horse swiftly down into the mountain draw and trotted silently along a snow-packed dry creek bed. He emerged into an opening in the forest just as the deer stepped from behind a tree about seventy-five yards to his left.

Lewis threw his hunting rifle up to his shoulder, took quick aim, and gently squeezed the trigger. His rifle belched fire and hurled its lead projectile down range. The ball struck the large doe directly behind its right front leg. The animal ran about fifty feet before it collapsed dead on the snowy forest floor.

Lewis smiled as he trotted his horse toward the bounty of over one hundred pounds of fresh meat for his family.

He smiled mused out loud, "I might just have to make me a new set of breeches and leggings out of that doe skin."

The Georgia and North Carolina men arrived in the Watauga settlements in the middle of the afternoon just two days after their first encampment in the mountains. They said their temporary farewells as they parted ways and headed off to their respective villages and cabins scattered throughout the mountains. Wappanakuk followed Robert along the narrow trail that led to the temporary home of the Hammock family.

"How far is it to your place, Robert?"

"Not far. Only about a half-hour to the west."

The time passed quickly. Wappanakuk asked Robert several other questions, but received only minimal responses. Robert was clearly in no mood to talk. Instead, he wrestled with his thoughts. He was excited to see his family again, but he dreaded it, as well. The news of Frank's death was a tremendous burden to bear. He was happy that Wappanakuk was with him. He hoped that the presence of an old friend might somehow ease the pain of the terrible news.

The two men crossed over a low ridge and soon a small cluster of cabins and outbuildings came into view. Robert headed in the direction of a large, older-looking cabin on the western edge of the settlement. The two men noticed a lot of activity around the cabin.

As they drew closer Robert was able to make out the faces of some of his boys. Robbie was chopping wood as Joshua stacked it against the cabin. John was tending a small fire that generated clouds of smoke. Strips of meat dangled from thin sticks suspended over the smoky fire. Nanye-Hi was on her knees working on a deer hide that was staked to the ground over a bed of leaves. She was scraping meat and tissue from the inside of the hide with a knife.

Joshua let out an excited yell and pointed. Robbie spun around to look. The older boy exclaimed, "Mother!" He dropped his axe and ran inside the cabin.

Joshua and John ran toward the approaching riders. Both boys exclaimed, "Papa!"

Robert eased his leg over the neck of his horse and slid stiffly from the saddle. He stomped both of his feet and tried to coax his sore back into straightening out so that he could stand upright. He had just about worked the stiffness out of his tired muscles and joints when the boys slammed into him at full speed. He hugged them as tears of joy filled his eyes and streamed down his face.

Soon the leaf-covered clearing beside the cabin was filled with children as they streamed out of the house and ran toward Robert. He waited eagerly for them to approach, but his eyes were focused on the cabin. He wanted to see his wife.

The moment that Milly emerged from the narrow door of the cabin he felt his spirit lift inside his breast. She flashed a broad smile that melted away months of blood, pain, suffering, hunger, and killing. There was life and love in her gaze.

His heart satisfied at the sight of his bride, Robert dropped down on one knee and accepted the overwhelming wave of children that washed over him. The sheer mass of the little ones soon knocked him over onto his back in the snow and leaves. Robert and the children all howled with delight. Wappanakuk laughed out loud at the family spectacle on display before him.

Milly approached more slowly. She carried Frank and Nanye-Hi's baby, Anna, on her hip. Nanye-Hi walked tentatively behind her, holding her son, Simeon, by the hand. When they reached the pile of family bedlam Milly handed the baby to Nanye-Hi and approached her husband. He climbed up off of the ground and dusted himself off. Milly slipped silently into his arms and placed her cheek against his chest. He reached his arms around her tightly and hugged her close.

"I missed you, Millenor Hammock."

"You need a bath, Robert Hammock."

Everyone laughed.

"And I see you brought an old friend with you." She looked up at Wappanakuk, who was still seated on his horse. "Wappanakuk, it is good to see you again."

"It is good to see you, as well, Miss Milly."

"Well, climb down off of that horse and make yourself at home. You two need to be fed, I'm sure. But you'll need to get washed first. You both smell like a field full of billy goats."

Robert heard his wife's words, but his heart and mind were focused on the face of Nanye-Hi. There was a sullen hollowness in her eyes. Robert sensed despair. It was almost as if she already knew.

Milly saw her husband staring at Nanye-Hi. She saw the agony on display in her husband's eyes. After seventeen years of marriage she was all too familiar with her husband's expressions. His face always betrayed what was in his heart. She stole a glance at Wappanakuk, who nodded very subtly and grimly.

"Robbie, take the children inside and have everyone wash up. We are going to have some treats. There is fresh sweet bread and jam inside."

"But Mama, Papa just got home. I want to talk …"

Milly interrupted him, "Do as I say, Robbie! Now! There will be plenty of time for you to talk to your father this evening. Take Simeon and Anna with you. We need some time to talk without any children around."

"Yes, Mama."

Robbie turned around and enlisted Joshua's help to corral all of the little ones and get them inside.

The moment that the cabin door closed Nanye-Hi stated solemnly and evenly, "My husband is dead."

Robert took her by the arm and tugged gently in the direction of the outdoor table. "Let's sit down over here and talk."

She jerked her arm away. "Robert, do not treat me like a child. Speak plainly to me. Frank is dead, isn't he?"

Robert looked her in the eyes. A single tear formed in his right eye. "Yes, Nanye-Hi. Frank is dead. He died in my arms at a place called Long Cane in South Carolina."

She nodded. "I knew that he was dead. I knew it in my spirit many weeks ago. I felt him leave me. I felt it in my belly … in the movements of the child that I carry. When did he die?" she asked.

"In early December, about eight weeks ago."

"It was in battle?"

Robert nodded gently. "He died along with thirteen other militiamen. When he was shot he was helping pull Colonel Elijah Clarke from the battlefield. We were in retreat. When he got hit I stayed with him and held him. I was there when he took his last breath."

"Then he died a good, brave death," she declared.

"Yes, Nanye-Hi. Yes he did. Frank was a gallant soldier. His fellow soldiers regarded him as such."

"And his body?" she asked.

"We buried him at the edge of the field where he fell, along with the thirteen other men from Georgia who died with him."

The young widow smiled at Robert. The smile dumbfounded him. It disturbed him. He could not understand how she could smile at him. He almost felt guilty for bringing her this horrible news.

"Robert, I am grateful for your care for my husband. He loved you very much. I think you know that. He died doing his duty and defending his people. No wife or mother could ask for or expect more. Now, if you will excuse me, I would like some time to myself for a while. Milly, will you watch my children for me for the remainder of the afternoon?"

Milly walked over to Nanye-Hi and wrapped her arms around her. "Of course, dear. You take all the time you want. We will be here when you are ready to return."

"Thank you, Milly."

The noble Cherokee girl turned and strolled toward the hill behind the cabin. The others watched in silence until she disappeared from view.

Milly turned to Robert. "I'm heartbroken over Frank. I know that it must have been horrible for you."

"It was rough at first, but I've had some time to work it all through in my mind. There was nothing that I could have done to make things any different. It was just his time, I suppose."

Milly took her husband by the hand and gave him a firm squeeze. "So, to change the subject ... how did you and Wappanakuk happen upon one another?"

"That's a long story. Let's save it for supper. Where's Lewis?"

"He's out on patrol for the militia. He should be back before dark."

"The men on the trail were telling me some amazing things about him. Turns out he's something of a legend around here. There's this pretty unbelievable story about him surviving a Cherokee attack and being shot full of arrows. Is that true?"

Milly grinned. "That's a long story, too. One for after supper. But first things first. You two aren't coming into my house without first sitting your hind parts in some hot, soapy water." She called to her sons, "Boys! Start heating water. We have a couple of stinky soldiers that we need to clean!"

Two hours later, just as dusk was descending over the mountains, Robert and Wappanakuk were freshly bathed and clad in clean clothes. Wappanakuk wore some of Robert's extra breeches and one of his homespun shirts. They were enjoying the warmth of the fireplace when they heard the crunch of a horse in front of the cabin.

"Lewis is back!" Robbie proclaimed. He ran to the door and threw it open. "He has a doe!" Robbie, Joshua, and John ran outside to help hang the animal on the limb of their butchering tree.

Robert left the door standing wide open. Everyone inside smiled as they listened to the young boys excitedly tell Lewis that his father and Wappanakuk were inside the house.

Seconds later Lewis came bounding through the door. He exclaimed, "Papa!" The boy, as big and brave as he was, ran to his father and wept in his arms.

And Wappanakuk was there, too! Lewis's heart leapt in his chest. He grabbed his Indian friend and gave him a huge hug. He was so happy that he thought he might explode!

The men had so many stories to tell! Robert and Lewis and Wappanakuk began to share excitedly about their battles and adventures. Of course, the news that Frank was dead took much of the joy and life out of the reunion, and it brought a new wave of tears from Lewis. He was heartbroken that he would never see his "big brother" Frank again

Milly cut their conversation short with her call to supper.

"You men-folk can talk all about your wars and fighting after supper. The food is hot, so let us eat."

"What about Nanye-Hi?" asked Robert. "She's still not back from her walk yet."

"She should not be out in the settlements after dark. There are some people around here who would give any excuse to put a bullet in an Indian. It's not safe for her," declared Lewis.

"I'll go and find her," volunteered Wappanakuk. "I do not believe she has gone far. You folks go ahead and eat. I will return with the girl as soon as I can."

"It's not safe for you out there, either," Lewis testified.

Wappanakuk smiled. "Do not worry about me, Tarowa Yetashta. I will be fine. Besides, I'm wearing some of your father's clothes. Don't I look just like a white settler?"

There was a moment of awkward silence and then everyone burst into laughter.

"Not exactly," commented Milly.

Wappanakuk grinned warmly. "Miss Milly, please keep us some food warm by the fire. I will return soon."

The Waccon warrior grabbed his weapons and exited swiftly. They heard the crunch of his moccasins in the snow for only a few steps and then the familiar silence of the mountains enveloped the cabin.

The family dived into their hot supper of rabbit and squirrel stew and salty corn cakes. The cabin was filled with laughter, joy, and conversation. Robert reveled in the love and warmth of his family. They told stories and sang songs for many hours until Milly declared that it was way past time for the little ones to go to bed. She herded them all into the far end of the cabin and pulled a makeshift curtain suspended on a leather thong that separated them from the adult side of the room.

The children soon drifted off to sleep and left the older folk in peace. Only Robbie and Lewis remained beside the fire with their mother and father. They continued their "catching up" and conversation for another couple of hours before finally giving in to fatigue and going to bed.

Robert's month of furlough passed quickly. His days with his family were wonderful, indeed. He hunted with his boys along the creeks and ridges of the mountains. He wrestled in the floor with the smaller boys and read and told stories to his girls in the evenings. Robert reveled in the peace and safety of their mountain retreat, but he knew that his days in Watauga were numbered. He would soon have to return to the war. It wasn't just duty that demanded his return. His heart also beckoned him to return and liberate his beloved Georgia from the stranglehold of the British.

February soon gave way to March, and the days began to warm just a little. There was still some snow on the ground, but it was easy to see that the death and gray of winter were beginning to yield to the life and green of spring. Robert's report date at Colonel Pickens' farm was March 15. For the sake of prudence and safety, Major Cunningham had informed the men that they needed to allow at least ten days for travel. They would depart on March 5. It was already March 3. Two days was all that Robert had left remaining of his winter retreat with his family.

That evening, following a hearty supper and fellowship around the family table, the adults, along with Lewis and Robbie, sat beside the fire and sipped hot tea with rum.

They talked about many wonderful and meaningful things. Milly snuggled beside her husband in a large chair. Wappanakuk sat on a stool. Nanye-Hi was beside him, and like the two teenage boys, sat cross-legged in the floor. Robert hated to cast a cloud upon their joyful moment, but he had to make his plans known.

"We have orders to report to Colonel Pickens' farm in the Long Cane District on March 15. I think you all know that."

Milly responded, "Yes, husband, we are all too aware of your coming departure. When do you plan to leave?"

"Sunup the day after tomorrow. We want to allow plenty of time for difficulty along the trail."

"That is wise to make plenty of time for travel," affirmed Wappanakuk. "Danger and difficulty abound in the mountains and hills of the Carolinas."

"I can go with you this time, Father!" chirped Lewis. "I'm ready to join the Regiment of Refugees!"

Robert shook his head. "No, son. I need you here with the family. Besides, the officers of the militia are counting on you for the defense of these mountains. You have responsibilities here, and here is where you belong. The men respect you here. I need you to stay."

"Yes, Father," Lewis responded.

Lewis understood his father's command and expectations. In fact, he was almost glad that his father had denied his request. He loved his job as a scout and Indian spy.

Silence ensued. Robert, Wappanakuk, and Lewis puffed on their pipes.

"What about you, Wappanakuk?" asked Milly. "Are you returning to your regiment?"

"No, Miss Milly. I have decided that it is time for me to return home. I have responsibilities to attend to there … a wife and children."

The Hammocks were flabbergasted. They had never heard a single word from Wappanakuk about a family.

"A wife and children?" exploded Robert. "You've never mentioned a wife and children! You've told us volumes about your brothers and sisters, and all about your cousins and uncles, but never a word about a wife and children!"

"That's because I do not have a wife and children yet," Wappanakuk remarked matter-of-factly.

Robert was more puzzled than ever. He looked at Milly, whose face also registered complete confusion.

"You are going to have to explain this to me, brother."

Wappanakuk glanced at Nanye-Hi. She lifted her hand and gently placed it on his knee. She smiled at him and then smiled at Milly and Robert.

"I will be returning with Wappanakuk to his home. I am to be his wife."

Robert was absolutely dumbfounded. His mouth hung wide open. Suddenly Milly shrieked with glee and began to clap her hands. It was a semi-silent shriek because she did not want to wake the children sleeping on the other side of the curtain. But her joy had to make its way out of her heart and into the room. She lunged toward Nanye-Hi, scooped her up off of the floor, and hugged her close.

"Oh, I am so happy for you, dear. It makes so much sense! I don't know why I didn't see it coming." Milly beamed with pleasure.

Robert's jaw was still on the floor. He hadn't even blinked since hearing Nanye-Hi's pronouncement.

"Robert, darling, you need to breathe," Milly teased.

He blinked and tried to clear the cobwebs from his brain. He muttered, "But ... but how? When? I don't understand ..."

"It is the answer to all of our needs, Robert," answered Wappanakuk. "Nanye-Hi does not fit here in this settlement. She has no ties of blood to your family. And she fears going home to her people because of the color and heritage of her children. But my people have been blended with whites and slaves for decades. Our culture is mixed. My people are open and welcoming. She will be most welcome in my village." He looked again at Nanye-Hi. "Besides, she is a beautiful and healthy young woman. Any man with reasonable intelligence would be thrilled to have her as his wife."

Nanye-Hi smiled broadly and blushed.

"What about her children?" asked Robert.

"I will raise them and treat them as my own. But they will know all about their brave father," Wappanakuk promised.

"The child within me will be born in three months. He will be called Frank, in honor of his father," added Nanye-Hi.

"What if it is a girl?" joked Robert.

Nanye-Hi looked at him in all seriousness and stated, "No, Robert. He is a boy."

Robert put up his hands in surrender, laughed, and nodded. "Well, then, it sounds like this is a done deal. You have decided."

"We have decided," answered both Wappanakuk and Nanye-Hi.

"Then I suppose congratulations are in order, my friend." Robert gave his Indian friend a hearty handshake.

"Will you be married here in Watauga?" asked Lewis.

"No. We will wait until we return to my people. I want us to have a Waccon wedding."

The Hammocks were all saddened.

"I wish that we could be there," replied Robert.

"I know, my friend. You will be with us in spirit, but you have more pressing matters to attend to than a wedding. You have a land to liberate and a home to reclaim."

Robert nodded. "Yes, old friend. Yes I do."

CHAPTER EIGHTEEN
WAR'S END

A gentle breeze blew up through the mountain pass. It cooled the sweat that covered Lewis's skin and soaked his shirt. It was only the second week of June, but the ample rains and high humidity gave the heavily wooded mountains an almost jungle-like feel. His nerves were on edge.

Lewis was, once again, on an extended patrol in search of the elusive Cherokee. He discovered that it was much harder to keep watch in the forests of the western wilderness of North Carolina during the warmer months. The thickening undergrowth and ample vegetation provided far too many places for the enemy to hide and set ambushes. He had to be extremely attentive and extra careful.

His discovery of evidence of an Indian camp just five miles from the settlements made his stomach churn. He had been tracking the Indians for the past two hours. They seemed to be heading toward the center of the Watauga villages.

Lewis snapped to attention as his hair bristled on his neck. He had caught a faint scent of Indians. It was a distinctively earthy aroma, originating from a mixture of dirt, smoke, and unwashed body odor. He knew that the natives were close by. A few minutes later he smelled smoke.

He saw a small cave cut into the hillside to his left. Lewis quickly and silently guided his horse toward the mouth of the cave. He tied the animal to a small tree that grew up against the steep hillside.

Lewis patted the animal on the neck and whispered into its ear, "I'll be right back, Molly. You stay put and don't make any noise."

The horse flicked its ears and gave him a nudge with her nose. Lewis scratched the pink skin of her nose and then turned and trotted off into the undergrowth. He moved stealthily and silently in his elk-hide pucker-toed moccasins. He slowly worked his way left along the hill toward its crest.

He froze in absolute stillness when he heard the murmuring of voices carrying over the top of the ridge. He squatted behind a tree, barely breathing, and listened to make sure that he had not been discovered. He heard the distinctive melody of the Cherokee language and an abundance of laughter.

"Good," he thought. "They don't suspect that I am here."

For the next fifteen minutes Lewis crept silently toward the top of the ridge. He was careful not to disturb a single twig or leaf. He attempted to melt into his surroundings and become part of the forest. He needed to know what these Cherokee were up to, and he had to remain undetected in order to spy on them.

Lewis's set his sights on a large rock that jutted out from the base of a huge hickory tree. He hoped that the narrow opening between the two would provide perfect cover for him and allow him to survey the Indians down below. Moments later he reached his goal. He removed his hat and ever-so-slowly raised up his head to peer over the top of the hill.

He gasped when he saw the Indians below. There were over twenty of them gathered near a slow-moving creek. They had two small fires burning and were roasting venison over the coals. The carcass of the deer lay on a large rock near the creek. Several of the Cherokee stood and munched on pieces the raw liver of the animal. Blood ran down their arms.

Their ponies were tied in a large cluster beside the water. The Indians were well-armed and obviously prepared for battle. This was a Cherokee raiding party. There could be no doubt about it. There were too many of them to simply be out hunting. They were headed for Watauga to take scalps and women.

"I have to get back and warn the militia!" Lewis thought.

He turned and eased back down the hill as quickly as he could. He knew that it was imperative that he remain silent as he evacuated the scene. These Cherokee would have no mercy on him.

Several minutes later he reached his mount. The horse nodded and pawed when she saw Lewis, but made no other noise.

Lewis patted her on the head. "Good girl," he whispered.

He walked and led the horse over a quarter of a mile … until he was well out of range of the Cherokee ears … then he mounted his horse and rode fast toward the settlements.

It was almost an hour later when Lewis topped the last ridge that led down into the Watauga villages. He drew to a stop on top of the ridge, pulled his first pistol and fired a warning shot. Thirty seconds later he pulled his other pistol and fired a second shot. He tucked both pistols back into his leather belt, snapped the reins, and yelled at his horse. The animal kicked into a hard run as she finished the last leg of her difficult journey.

Lewis heard bells ringing the alarm as he emerged into the center of the main town. Colonel John Sevier and several of his officers were gathered there. Lewis slid his horse to a stop in front of them. Other men began to gather around.

"What is it Lewis?" asked the colonel. "Why the alarm?"

Lewis jumped down off of his horse. "Sir, I tracked and spied on a Cherokee war party to the south."

"How far out?" asked the colonel.

"Less than five miles."

The colonel's eyes grew wide. "That close? How many?"

"I counted two dozen of them sir, all armed for battle."

"Did you get close enough to make sure?"

Lewis smiled. "I spied on them from the ridge just above. I was about thirty yards from them."

The militiamen smiled and nodded. The colonel grinned. "That close, huh?"

Lewis nodded humbly. "Give or take. I was close enough to smell their stinky armpits."

The men gathered around laughed.

"What were they doing?" asked the colonel.

"They were cooking and eating, sir. They had a small doe skinned beside a creek and were roasting venison. They didn't appear to be in a hurry to me. They were in high spirits, laughing and conversing. And they were well-armed. There were rifles, pistols, and bows strapped all over their ponies. It's a war party, sure enough."

"Excellent report, scout. You've given us the advantage of surprise. We'll take it from here. The militia will be assembled and on the move within the hour. You just head on home and get some hot food and rest. We'll let you know when our men return."

"Yes, sir. I'm a might bit tired and hungry. I've been out in the woods for three days."

Colonel Sevier patted Lewis on the shoulder. "You're a good scout, Mr. Hammock. I wish you would think about staying here with us when your folks go back to Georgia."

Lewis grinned. "I promise I'll think about it, sir."

"Excellent. Now get. I'll see you in a few days."

"Thank you, sir."

Lewis trotted over to his horse and climbed up into the saddle. He pointed her toward the west and headed for his cabin and some of his mama's home cooking.

It was late on a June afternoon. Robert knew that he was getting closer to his family's mountain cabin in Watauga. He was ecstatic about seeing them again. Just three months earlier he had departed these mountains to return to the war. He was determined to fight until Georgia was liberated from the British. He was determined to take his family back home.

Now those events, which only a short time ago seemed like remote, distant possibilities, had become reality. Robert and Georgia's Regiment of Refugees had taken part in the siege and liberation of Augusta. The Tory Colonel "Burnfoot" Brown had been defeated. The British and Tories had fled the backcountry and they were barely hanging on to Savannah and the areas along the coast.

The Regiment of Refugees was disbanded. Many of the men had already returned to their frontier homes. Many others, like Robert, were headed to Watauga to get their families.

Robert had finally reached the mountains. He knew

that he was only minutes away from Milly and the children. His heart felt lighter with each step of his trusty horse. How surprised they would all be! He was guiding his horse through a narrow, dry creek bed when he heard movement to his left. He swiftly drew his horse to a stop and hid behind the trunk of a large tree.

He listened carefully and heard the sound of another horse. He drew a pistol from his belt and quietly pulled the hammer back to full cock, then gently tilted his head to the right to peek from behind the tree.

The sound of the other horse stopped. Robert knew that he had been discovered. His heart raced as he scanned the woods for some sign of another human. He jumped just a bit when he saw a set of eyes peering at him from behind a large boulder.

But they were very familiar eyes.

And then there was a familiar voice. "Papa?" the voice exclaimed.

It was Lewis!

Robert's face broke into a huge smile as he released the cock on his pistol and tucked it back into his belt. He guided his horse from behind the tree. He and Lewis met in the center of the gravel creek bed. Both men jumped from their horses and embraced one another.

"Lewis, what are you doing wandering around in the woods by yourself?"

"I just got back off of a long-range patrol. I found a Cherokee war party five miles to the southwest and just now made my report to Colonel Sevier. I'm headed back home now to rest up and get some food."

"You were out by yourself?"

"Yes, sir. We Indian spies work alone." He grinned broadly. "What are you doing home so soon? Mama is going to have a fit!"

"It's over, son. Brown surrendered Augusta. The British are in Savannah now and likely leaving Georgia altogether. There's peace on the frontier. The Creeks have moved west. Georgia is free!"

"So we're going home now?" asked Lewis.

"Yes, son. It is safe now. We can go home."

Lewis grinned. "Let's go tell Mama!"

It was about a half-hour before sunset when Robert and Lewis came over the low ridge to the east of the cabin. The entire family was outside, enjoying the cool shade provided by the high canopy of trees. Robert smiled when he saw his beautiful wife sitting on a stool and leaning back against the wall of the cabin. Her bonnet was off and he could see her shiny, auburn hair.

Some of the children saw the riders approaching and cautiously watched them move down the trail, unsure about who was riding beside Lewis. When they were about thirty yards from the house Robert heard his son Joshua squeal, "It's Papa! Mama! Robbie! John! It's Lewis and he's found Papa!"

That word, "Papa," traveled like wildfire among the children. All of them burst into screaming, "Papa! Papa! Papa!"

The entire family took off running toward them. Even Milly ran to meet her husband. They met at the spot where the trail met the clearing beside the cabin. Robert jumped from his horse and tumbled into the arms of his family. They covered him with hugs and kisses. Milly fought her way through the crowd of squealing children to get her turn. She wrapped her arms around her husband's strong neck. He lifted her up off of the ground and hugged her close.

"Why are you back so soon?" she asked. "It's only been three months. Did you get another furlough?"

Robert grinned and kissed his wife on the lips.

"No, my love. It's over."

"You mean the war is over?" she exclaimed.

"Well, ours is." He smiled broadly. "Augusta is liberated. Brown has surrendered. The Tories are all gone from the backcountry. Their militiamen are in prison in South Carolina."

"What are we going to do now?" asked Milly.

"We are going home, my love. That is what we are going to do. We are going home to Georgia ... for good."

Three days later the Hammock family packed all of their belongings on their horses and began their trek back to Georgia.

Three months later the Patriot armies and the French navy cornered General Lord Cornwallis and the British armies at a place called Yorktown, Virginia. Cornwallis surrendered. The war was over.

Then the British began their trek back to England, leaving the United States in freedom and in peace.

THE REAL LEWIS HAMMOCK AND HIS FAMILY

Most of the central characters in this story were real people. Some, but not all, of the peripheral characters were real, as well. I attempted to develop their personalities as I interpreted them across two hundred and fifty years of time. I hope that I did them justice.

Robert Hammock II (1737-1799) was my 5th great-grandfather through my father's mother's family line. This novel blends the truths of his history with the "literary license" of historical fiction. His service in the Regiment of Refugees of Richmond County is well-documented, and he is a recognized Patriot of the American Revolution by both the Daughters and the Sons of the American Revolution. After the war he brought his family back to Georgia and resettled his original headright lands. He also received additional acreage as a bounty for his service in the Revolution. Robert Hammock became a modest planter in northern Georgia and died there in 1799. His son, Lewis, was executor of his estate.

Millenor Jackson Hammock survived her husband and lived to the ripe old age of ninety-two, dying in Georgia in 1832. She received acreage from the state of Georgia in a land lottery for widows of Revolutionary War veterans in the early 1800's. In 2015 I had her recognized by the Sons of the American Revolution for her Patriotic Service. She swore a deposition in the Georgia Indian Depredation Claims in the 1820's in which she described an Indian attack upon her family's household and the loss of some horses. That testimony, combined with her husband's status as a Refugee soldier, provided sufficient evidence of her Patriotic Service.

Lewis Hammock was my fourth great-grandfather. Though I have examined every document that I can possibly find, I cannot locate any evidence of his service in the Revolution. However, he served in the Wilkes County Militia in September 1793 as a sergeant and commanded a detachment in the frontier wars against the Creek Indians. His brother, Joshua, served as a private in his unit. The fact that he served as a sergeant in that conflict would seem to indicate that he had prior military service, most likely in a partisan unit during the Revolution.

The last individual that I want to address from my story is the slave named Frank. The entire story line that centers on Frank in this novel is fictitious in its entirety. However, Frank was actually a real person. There is only one documentary record that exists which named Frank. Robert Hammock did, indeed, inherit "a negro boy named Frank" from his maternal grandfather, William Hugh Lambert, in 1765 ... the same year that Lewis Hammock was born. Since no other record exists that mentions Frank, I took the liberty of building a story around him that would honor the slaves and other men of color who faithfully and valiantly served the Patriot cause in the American Revolution.

It has been my honor and joy to explore the history of these great Patriots and to share with you what might have been their story.

Geoff Baggett

REVOLUTIONARY WAR GLOSSARY

Breeches – These were the pants of the colonial period. They were secured with buttons and baggy in the seat. The pants reached just below the knee. Men typically wore long socks that covered their lower leg and extended up over the knee.

Brown Bess – This is the name given to the British Army's military musket. They were mass-produced, smooth-barreled flintlock weapons that fired a .75 caliber (¾ inch) round lead ball.

Charlestown – The colonial name of Charleston, South Carolina. It was founded in 1670 and named after King Charles II of England.

Continental Army – Soldiers in the federal army of the United States as authorized by the Continental Congress.

Dragoons – A special type of soldier in the British army. They were "mounted infantry" who could either fight on horseback or on foot.

English Saddle - These were typical horse saddles used before the development of the western saddle. These older saddles did not have a saddle horn, which was used in the western United States in roping cattle. Instead, they had a small hump between the knees of the rider that was known as the "pommel."

Flintlock – The type of weapons, loaded through the muzzle, used during the American Revolution.

Ford – A shallow place in a river that provided good footing so that travelers could walk across on the river bottom rather than swimming or being ferried across.

Freedmen – Former slaves who were set free by their masters.

Freedom Papers – Special documents given to freedmen by their former masters. These documents proved the free status of those who held them and served as insurance against any accusation of being a runaway slave.

Frizzen – The part of a flintlock weapon that the flint strikes to make a spark and ignite the gunpowder.

Gallows – Structures used for the execution of criminals by hanging.

Huzzah – A joyful shout, and the early form of the modern word, "hoorah," or "hooray."

Indentured Servitude – This was a form of "voluntary slavery" in which poor people signed over their freedom to wealthy people for a set period of time. In return for their years of servitude they earned something such as passage by ship to America, the learning of a work trade, or shelter and food.

Indian – A traditional term used to refer to Native Americans. The term arose out of the confusion of early explorers. When they arrived in the Americas they thought that they had reached the east coast of India. Therefore they referred to the native peoples as "Indians." The name "stuck" and became a word of common use in the United States.

Injun – The slang word for "Indian."

King's Highway – The British east coast highway that ran all the way from Boston to Charleston. It was later extended to Savannah, Georgia.

Leggings – Also known as "**Gaiters**," these were protective garments for the lower legs. They were often made of wool, canvas, cotton, or animal skins. They were secured with buttons or straps and served to protect and insulate the exposed lower leg between the breeches and shoes.

Litter – A makeshift vehicle used to transport sick or wounded soldiers. It was often made of cloth or animal skins suspended between two poles. It could be carried by people on foot or dragged behind a horse.

Livery – A business found in many towns that served the owners of horses. Also known as a livery stable, it was a place where a person could secure food, care, and housing for their horses overnight.

Loyalist – A citizen of the American colonies loyal to King George III and Great Britain.

Militia – Local county and state military units. Most served locally. There were both Patriot and Loyalist militia units during the war.

Muster – The official forming of local militia units for mobilization in the war.

Neck Sock – A garment that resembled a necktie. It was made of a long piece of cloth that was wrapped around the neck and then tied in a decorative fashion in the front.

Palisades – Walls made from upright stakes or tree trunks that were often pointed on top. They were built for defense, such as in the walls of primitive forts.

Patriots – People in American who were in favor of separation from England and the formation of a separate country.

Pipe Tomahawk – A tomahawk that contained a smoking bowl on the back of the blade and a hollow tube through the length of the handle. Smokers could ignite their tobacco in the bowl and smoke it by sucking on a mouthpiece on the end of the handle. It was often used for ceremonial purposes.

Pipe Tongs – A simple metal tool, similar to tiny salad tongs, that was used to pick up a small coal from a campfire or fireplace. Smokers would use the coal in pipe tongs to light their pipes.

Pommel – The small hump on the front of a saddle.

Pucker-toed Moccasins – Typical lightweight moccasins of the Eastern Woodland Indians. Made from animal hides, each moccasin had a thread that was pulled through the leather on top which caused it to have its distinguishing "pucker."

Queue – Pronounced "kew." This is the word for a man's pony tail. Men in Colonial times wore their hair long. They would often tie it in the back or braid it into a queue.

Redcoats – The derogatory name that Patriots called British soldiers.

Spectacles – The old name for eyeglasses.

Shilling – An old form of British coin money. It was worth 1/20 of a British Pound Sterling, and the equivalent of twelve pence.

Sons of Liberty – A secret society in the American colonies that was formed to protect the rights of American colonists and protest against unfair taxation by the British.

Station – Another name for a frontier fort.

Swamp Fever – The old word for the modern mosquito-borne disease known as malaria.

Tory / Tories – Another name for Loyalists.

Weskit – Also known as a **waistcoat**, this was the vest worn over the top of a man's shirt and under a man's coat. It would sometimes be worn without the outer overcoat. It was a more formal outer garment.

ABOUT THE AUTHOR

Geoff Baggett is a small town pastor in rural Kentucky. Though his formal education and degrees are in the fields of chemistry, biology, and Christian theology, his hobbies  and obsessions (according to his wife) are genealogy and Revolutionary War history. He is an active member of the Sons of the American Revolution and has discovered over twenty Patriot ancestors in his family tree from the states of Virginia, North and South Carolina, and Georgia.

Geoff is an avid living historian, appearing regularly in period uniform in classrooms, reenactments, and other Revolutionary War commemorative events throughout the southeastern United States. He lives on a small piece of land in rural Trigg County, Kentucky, with his amazing wife, a daughter and grandson, and a yard full of fruit trees and perpetually hungry chickens and goats.

Made in the USA
Lexington, KY
12 September 2019